A LESSON IN COWBOYS AND MURDER

DAVID UNGER, PHD

Artwork by Damonza
ISBN-13:978-1-7323395-3-8

Author Note

One of the challenges I faced writing about the 80s is that many of the things we now hold as fundamental values were not in place at the time. I have endeavored to have my characters hold respect for others in the forefront of their interactions, but wanted to stay true to the tenor of the times. Their actions and words might not always be as sensitive as they could be, but historic wrongs can only be righted if we acknowledge them. Where they appear here, they are a deliberately mindful reminder of how far we've come ... and how far we still have to go.

"Cowboy work is more than a job; it is a life-style and a medium of expression."

John R Erickson

PROLOGUE

"THE BEST EVER? That's a tough one."

"It's not that tough. Come on. Tell me."

"Are we talking movies, singers, TV? What?"

"I don't care. You could include rodeos, on the range, or yodeling in the shower."

"Well, I do occasionally yodel in the shower, but I don't reckon anyone else would include that in their best-of list."

"That's a safe bet, but come on, who's your all-time number-one cowboy?"

Yes, I was eavesdropping, but I wasn't really all that interested in who the guys in front of me deemed the best all-time cowboy. You and I might be able to name some contenders, but this best-ever thing was getting old.

How many conferences, festivals, adult fantasy camps am I going to go to where people are having these same discussions? I'm hoping many more, but you'd think people would have other things to talk about while they're standing in line. Still, here I was in the registration line for the inaugural Cowboy Poetry Gathering in Elko, Nevada, and people were putting together their best-ever lists.

I'm not a big cowboy fan. I was out of my element. It didn't take me long to notice I was the only person in the line not wearing cowboy boots. Most had the hat, too.

Cowboys are one thing. Poetry is another. I'm not a big poetry guy either. I enjoy it when it's put to music, but I still have scars from my poetry-writing attempts in English class.

So, what was I doing in Elko in January with the falling snow, my marginal interest, and my questionable fashion sense?

I was working. I'd been invited to be one of the "attractions." This was a new thing for me. My books have earned me a bit of a reputation and I, along with some others, had been asked to participate in a "semi-improvisational, partially scripted" show to close the event.

One of the people connected to the Gathering had been at the mystery writers' conference in Vegas where I'd dressed up like Agatha Christie's Hercule Poirot and helped solve a few murders. Boots Sarandon had determined I'd give his show a certain flair and wanted me to be one of the actors. He obviously hadn't done any investigative work into my thespian skills.

CHAPTER ONE

THE BACKSTORY

ASIDE FROM TEACHING graduate students how to do therapy, I'm also a practicing therapist. More and more, I'm becoming an out-of-the-box therapist. I used to mostly see people in my office, but now I often get asked to help out in the real world. As you well know, the real world is not all we'd like it to be.

These last years, I've been to a music festival with a client, a mystery writers' conference with a client, and the Dodgers Adult Baseball Fantasy Camp with a quasi-client. I'd also attended a therapist conference for some professional development credits that enabled me to keep my license.

At every one of those events, someone got murdered and I was able to put what skills I have to practical use and figure out whodunit.

I've learned numerous things from my experiences. First and foremost, I needed to have a gumshoe travel kit. So far, it contains a flashlight and extra cash. That's it. No doubt there are other things I could throw in, but I had other concerns as I packed.

It was January, which among other things meant school was in session. I don't like to miss class. I didn't mind it when I was a student, but as a teacher I find it less appealing. I'd skipped a week in October to go to the Dodger camp, and now I'd skip a second.

I'd asked the same former student to sub for me as she'd gotten rave reviews so I didn't think it would raise administrative concerns, but I'd need to stay under their radar the rest of the year.

Boots Sarandon had contacted me a week earlier about being one of the "attractions" at the inaugural Gathering. He'd apologized for the last-minute invite but flattered me sufficiently that I was willing to rearrange my schedule. I'd told him I'd feel out of place at a cowboy poetry event, being neither cowboy nor poet, but he'd said that while there were going to be some true poets in attendance, most everyone else was more a storyteller. Plus, Hal Cannon, the primary organizer, wanted to draw in other "arty types" and Boots imagined I'd appeal to a certain group. I was afraid to ask which one. While he'd not been impressed with my impression of Hercule Poirot, my ability to command center stage and weed out the killer had garnered his attention, and he was hoping I'd bring a certain *je ne sais quoi* to the finale he was planning.

Boots was going to have the cast perform "highlights" of the week in an interactive, spontaneous, and yet somewhat scripted show. He wanted me to play the part of a New England preppie dropout who'd gone on to become something of a wiz in the advertising business. At least I didn't have to mangle a Belgian accent.

The cast would meet each night for dinner and review the day's highlights. He'd put together the script as we went along and hand it over to us on the last day. We'd all stand on stage in a row and read the scripts as if we were on an old radio show. Periodically there'd be moments for spontaneous interaction, but we'd have to wait and see about those.

I wasn't sure what "spontaneous interaction" meant, but it could fun. And, of course, once the murders started, that was enough to rope me in.

CHAPTER TWO

TO GET THERE YOU HAVE TO GO HERE

You ever been to Elko, Nevada? Probably not. I hadn't. Turns out it's not easy to get there. Well, it may be for you. For me, there were no flights or trains. I had to go to the Automobile Club to get a map to chart out how to get there. Where I come from, we'd say Elko is in the middle of nowhere. Which, I suppose, is where it wants to be.

To travel the 700 miles from Los Angeles to Elko, you basically have two choices. You can drive to Las Vegas, try not to lose all your money, and wake up the next day sober enough to drive north 400 miles. Or you can head north to San Francisco, eat a first-rate meal, and drive east from there. If you do that, the person at the Automobile Club told me, you'd have to drive "the loneliest highway in the world." Want to guess which option I took?

The representative at the Automobile Club also gave me a solid piece of advice. The average January temperature in Elko is in the mid-thirties. That's the high. The low is in the teens. Left to my own devices, I'd have presumed it's Nevada—I'll bring T-shirts, jeans, a couple of button-down shirts, and my dark blazer. Now I had to throw in sweaters, jackets, and other layers of clothing that would still render me cold.

Car travel time can be a plus or minus thing. There's scenery to see, thoughts to wander, and obscure radio stations to listen to. If you've spent any time with me, you'll know I'm not a big practitioner of foreplay. Travel time is a close relative of foreplay. It's what you do in order to get to do what you want to do. As with other forms of foreplay, I try to be a good sport about it, but given the choice just teleport me there already.

Once I made the decision to stop in Vegas, several scenarios crossed my mind. I could go to a buffet and make a pig of myself. I could try to hit a jackpot and forever alter my life. I could visit Lucky, and possibly even Louise. Maybe in reverse order.

When I was in college, I became familiar with CliffsNotes. I like to think there was an "A" student named Cliff whose friend copied his notes and made a living for himself. Neither Cliff nor his friend are handy, so I'm going to briefly introduce you to some of the people I met during my last visit to Vegas.

Lucky and Louise. Lucky's a cab driver who became the Tonto to my Lone Ranger. He wouldn't take kindly to that description, but this is a cowboy story. I ran into him again in Vero Beach. The last time I saw him he was going to take a box of baseballs we'd found and investigate a career change.

As for Louise, it's complicated. There was a lot going on with her. Crystal Aplenty was her stage name. Most likely adopted when she became an exotic dancer or a brothel owner. She was not a romantic interest of mine, although when you do what she does for a living and look like she does, other interests surface. While my other interests were interested, I was mostly interested in discovering if she was also a murderer.

I remembered the name of the establishment where Louise oversaw people's momentary escapes. I also had Lucky's beeper number, though I didn't know if he was back in the cab business in Vegas.

He may have followed through on opening up a detective agency in Florida and be interested in finding out how long it would take to get to Elko.

CHAPTER THREE

VEGAS, BABY

MY PLAN WAS: one night in Vegas, five nights in Elko, then back to Vegas for an additional one-nighter. I'm not a big Vegas guy. Most people go there with hope and come back with less. I don't know how your life's going but for most of us an infusion of significant bucks would be an add-on. Vegas gives you that hope. Then dashes it.

Driving there I had hope.

Lucky told me he was settled in Vero Beach and wouldn't be able to make it to Elko. I was hoping he'd show up, but cowboys and poetry hold about the same allure for him as they do for me. He'd managed to parlay his baseball collection into creating his own detective agency, but his past exploits precluded him from acquiring a private investigator's license. As he explained it to me, he had to become a public investigator.

I know next to nothing about what a private investigator's license allows you to do, but I'm sure it allows you to call yourself a PI. Lucky decided to call himself a public investigator so when people asked what he did, he'd say, "I'm a PI."

Louise was another thing. When I finally got hold of her, she suggested we meet at the scene of the crime and have dinner at the Sands Hotel. Since that's where I'd booked a room, it worked for me, but it would put a crimp in my buffet behavior, which my heart and waist ought to appreciate if not my gluttony.

I met her in the lobby at seven.

For those of you who don't recall or have never met her, she was built like a brick shithouse. Tall and statuesque with long black hair.

She was still tall and statuesque but now she was a platinum blonde. Her fashion sense hadn't changed—low-cut, form-fitting black leather mini dress, above-the-knee black boots—and she'd retained her fetching look.

She gave me a full-on hug, reminding me that even if her breasts weren't real, they were present and accounted for.

"Hi there, stranger," she said. "Welcome back."

"While it's not great to be back, it's a pleasure seeing you. You look like a good time."

"I aim to please."

"Well, you certainly are an eyeful."

"And a handful."

"That too. You ready to eat?"

"Us working girls usually avoid the buffets, but this being a special occasion, bring it on."

She brought it on. While I tried to exhibit some restraint, reluctance was the only thing not on her plate. I let her dismantle a couple of crab legs before I took out the note.

"Louise, let me remind you what you wrote me the last time I was here."

She licked her fingers in a way that made me wonder. Once she was done teasing me and cleaning herself, she read it aloud.

Hercule,

I liked your friend until he dumped me in a laundry basket. Never had that happen before. I imagine you have figured out that while you thought you'd invited me to the whodunit, it was Poe's plan to have you bring me. He had a backup plan in case

you didn't, but he was pretty sure you would. He's a sly fellow.
I enjoyed playing the game. I heard someone confessed to the
murders so that's good news, but a confession does not a killer
make.

Crystal

PS: When you're back in Vegas, drop by.

"I presume you don't call yourself Hercule anymore."

"Yeah, that never really fit me well. You still call yourself Crystal?"

"Now and then. You still hang out with that dildo client of yours?"

"I'm afraid that's privileged information."

"So be it. If you see him, tell him he owes me an apology. Not that I'd accept it, but it's overdue."

"If I see him, I'll pass that along. But I've got a question for you. You wrote *a confession does not a killer make.* You want to tell me more about that?"

"That would go in the privileged information category."

Now, I have to stop here because that set up a dilemma I've faced before. I could suggest she hire me as her therapist, at which point her privileged information would become my own. But if I did that, any dreams of following up on her finger-licking would remain a fantasy.

As you may be aware, I've yet to write a decent sex scene. I blame it on not having a decent sex scene. Yet. A sexual encounter with Louise would surely be more than decent. But, as I asked myself in Vero Beach, *Would I have sex with someone just so I could write about it?* In Vero Beach I'd been saved from having to answer that because the person I was considering having sex with wasn't considering having sex with me.

Louise, however, might be more open to it. Then again, when you screw people for a living, you're apt to be pickier about who you do it with in your private life. I wasn't positive Louise screwed people for a living, but I had visited her Marquis de Sade office, where she whipped people for a living. With no interest in being on the receiving end of any more whips, I wasn't sure how to proceed.

"What's the matter, sugar? I can see those gray cells jostling all over the place."

"Very observant. I'm debating how curious I am about that privileged information."

"Let me make it easy for you. I'm not the kind of girl to kiss and tell."

"Does that mean you're not the kind of girl to murder and tell?"

"Honey, if I were, I wouldn't be here."

"One more thing and then you can get back to the crab legs. If you were the kind of girl who now and then murdered, have you gotten that out of your system?"

"You better hope so."

I'm going to leave the *did we or didn't we* till later. What's the point of a mystery if you don't have some mystery?

I don't usually mess with you this way, especially being mostly an advocate for truth-telling. So here's a truth. The reason I'm not telling is because this is not the last we're going to hear about Louise. And the even greater truth is, if we have to wait for the murders to happen, the least I can do is give you something to chew on.

CHAPTER FOUR

ELKO, NEVADA

Sunday January 27, 1985

I'VE BEEN DOWN this trail before, I observed as I saddled up my car and drove off.

You like to drive long distances in the desert? Some do. Me, not so much. I favor more visual stimulation, yet when you focus more you do notice nuances. I'm not good at that but had plenty of time to build my skills.

I don't know why Elko was chosen as the site for the Gathering. Maybe they were hoping for a small meet; although when I asked a friend if he'd ever heard of the place, he said it was the last real cowboy town in the West. That could explain it.

Not that I hold what Hunter Thompson writes as gospel, but this is what he said about Elko: "The federal government owns 90% of this land, and most of it is useless for anything except weapons testing and poison-gas experiments." Reading that didn't build up my excitement level.

Elko was nestled below a mountain range and had the Humboldt River running close by. The natural surroundings upped the aesthetics, but postcard-worthy it wasn't. I just wanted the poisonous gases to have moved along.

My lodgings were well-established in the town's history. I, along with the other "attractions," was staying at Stockmen's Hotel and Casino. Apparently, it's the classiest place in town. Like a lot of things, that's relative.

When you're staying in the last real cowboy town, with a population of ten thousand, you need to temper your expectations. I try not to be too much of a city boy, but I am. Still, I had my own bathroom and a balcony, so I'll save my complaining for other matters.

I'd reached Elko late in the afternoon. Tomorrow was the first full day of activities. Tonight, I was meeting Boots and the rest of the cast for dinner at Stockmen's restaurant.

CHAPTER FIVE

CAST DINNER

I HAVE A thing about time. If you and I were due to meet someplace at six thirty, I'd be there at six fifteen and get irritated with you at six thirty-five, and annoyed at six forty. Anything beyond that and I'd be cranky. But that's about you and me. If it's a larger social thing, I don't want to be early. I have social skills. I can make small talk but I don't seek it out. I prefer to arrive late.

I'm a therapist. I sit with people while they vent their emotions and endeavor to speak their truth. Small talk doesn't usually flourish. Often you have to go through the small talk to get to the big talk but, as you know, foreplay ain't my thing.

I arrived at six forty-five. There were six people at the table.

A lanky, weathered forty-something guy came over to greet me.

"Howdy, Dr. Unger. I'm Boots Sarandon and it's my privilege to meet you in person."

"Hi, Boots. I recognize you from the mystery writers' conference, but we never got to meet. I'm glad to be here and looking forward to the week."

"I can't wait to sit and chew the fat about your books, but first I want to introduce you to the folks," he said as he led me to the table.

"Everybody, this is Dr. Unger, or Slick as he'll be known to you. Let's all introduce ourselves with our first names and our stage names."

"I'm Eileen," said a straight-laced, attractive older woman with big hair. "But you can call me Dale, Dale Evans."

"Hello, Dale."

"I'm Jason," said an unshaven man in his thirties. "The Lone Ranger."

"Call him Lone," said Boots.

"Will do."

Next up was an early-forties man who didn't seem pleased to be there. "I'm Nathaniel, but best, pilgrim, if you call me Duke, aka John Wayne," he said, and sounded like the real thing.

"Will do. I don't want to mess with you."

"I'm Laura. You can call me Cat. Cat Ballou."

"Cat, I'll be more than happy to do that."

Jeez. I'd just met the woman and I was already flirting with her in front of other people.

"And I'm Bill," said a wiry steely-eyed man, "but you can call me Roy. Roy Rogers."

"Roy, it's a pleasure to meet you as well."

"There you go," said Boots. "Grab a seat and hunker down."

I wanted to sit next to Cat but Duke and Roy had already taken those seats. Being a good sport, I sat down next to Dale.

"Hi, Dale. Want to tell me about yourself and why Boots asked you to join our ensemble?"

"Certainly, but not before I tell you that I'm a fan of your books, though to tell you the truth, they're a bit much."

"If you're looking for an argument, you won't get one here. Frankly, Dale, I'm a bit much myself."

"You certainly are. When I heard you were going to be with us I was delighted. I've got all sorts of questions for you," she said, inching forward.

"I asked first. I'm sure Boots wanted you here for reasons other than your curiosity."

"All of us here are storytellers and cowboys. You're a storyteller but you ain't no cowboy. You're the outsider."

"Is that a good thing or a bad thing?"

"Depends who you ask. It's a good thing if you're partial to anomalies. It isn't if you're not."

"I tend to have my own understanding of what words mean. But *anomaly* has a certain negative spin. It's a deviation. Are you someone who prefers things more standardized?"

"There you got me. I was a teacher for a spell and relied on standardized tests."

We've been told that cultivating gratitude is key to living a happier life. I was grateful when Boots stood up and strode toward a late-fifties hombre decked in a floppy cowboy hat and a brown duster.

We all watched as there were pats on the back that substitute for hugs in some quarters. After a short exchange, Boots escorted him to the table.

"Ladies and gentlemen, I'm proud to introduce this range-riding, cow-busting, rip-roaring cowboy to you. This here is Clay, who you'll come to know better as Buffalo Bill."

Boots was into typecasting. Buffalo Bill was carrying some extra weight and didn't look to be the type you could budge. I'd once been in Yellowstone when a herd of buffalo chose to lounge on the highway. As long as they were lounging, so were the cars. Buffalo Bill had that same look—the kind of person who did what he wanted when he wanted.

The introductions were interrupted when two people ran up to Boots and whispered to him. He stared out at the entrance, excused himself, and hightailed it out of the room.

Things were still while we waited.

Soon Boots ran back over to us.

"There's been a horrible accident. Annie Oakley and Gene Autry went up to Hopalong Cassidy's room. The radio was loudly playing and they knocked and knocked, but there was no answer. They got someone to open the door and found him shot dead on the bed."

Let the murders begin …

CHAPTER SIX

AFTER DINNER

THERE ARE PROBLEMS ahead. We've had them before and dealt with them so we can again. A recurring one for me is names. People have them. They prefer it when you remember them. Unfortunately, that's a skill set I've not fully developed. If you relate to that, help is at hand. From here on, I'm going to call the cast members by their stage names, and only the first ones at that. So here's who we've got so far: Boots, Duke, Lone, Cat, Buffalo, Dale, Roy, and Hopalong, now deceased. We also have Annie and Gene, who discovered Hopalong but whom we've yet to meet. And of course me, Slick.

Dinner was a glum affair. While we were all sad to hear about Hopalong, none of us aside from Boots had known him. Still, any anticipatory excitement we shared was under wraps. I was debating dessert when Boots stood up, put on his hat, and came over to me.

"Can I have a private word with you?" he said as he headed out of the restaurant.

"Certainly," I said, catching up. "But first, what's the story with your hat? It's different than the others I've seen."

"Custom-made. Next to my horse, it's my best friend."

"You've got a fitting friend."

"Thanks. Now, follow me."

We took the stairs to the second floor. A couple of police officers and several others stood in and out of what must have been Hopalong's room.

"They won't let us in there, but let's walk by and see what we can see."

I got a glimpse of Hopalong's legs and cowboy boots at the end of the bed.

Then Boots said, "My room's over here. I'd have heard if he'd been shot when I was inside."

"Yeah, the walls here weren't built for privacy."

We went to the end of the hall and turned back. I didn't see anything new on the return journey.

"Why'd we do that?"

"I need to be honest with you."

"You don't have to be, but it might help."

"I was worried there'd be bad blood spilled this week. I realize I told you that I wanted you in the show for your storytelling, but I brought you here under false pretenses, and for that I apologize."

"Want to tell me why you did bring me here?"

"For this," he said, pointing down the hall. "I couldn't bring in a legit detective as that would have scared everyone off. It's not like we're dealing with a totally law-abiding crowd here. But if I told them I'd seen you in Vegas and you'd be an easy outsider to lampoon, they'd go for it. I know that doesn't sound right, but it's the truth. We don't cotton to strangers, but you can take it."

"I'm not sure that was a compliment, but okay. Dale said I was an anomaly, so I get it. You thought I was an anomaly they could stomach."

"Not entirely. If you don't mind my saying so, you're not that easy to stomach. But I had a hunch you could stomach it. And while you're doing that, you can figure out who's spilling the blood."

"Wait a minute. You knew someone was going to be killed so

you brought me in to be the butt of people's distaste for outsiders, and work out whodunit?"

"Yes and no. Yes, I brought you in to work out whodunit … if there was a whodunit. But, no, I didn't know someone was going to be killed. I suspected it. I also suspect we're in for more murder. Maybe something else as well."

"Something else as well?"

"That could be good or bad news. I don't know. I just know we got a gold rush now in Elko and we've got more whorehouses than we do churches. This might be the mystery where you strike it rich and get to write that sex scene."

CHAPTER SEVEN

REHEARSAL

When Boots and I got back to the dining room he hurried over to someone I hadn't seen before.

"Everyone," said Boots. "This good-looking, rugged rodeo star is Phil Marcoe, who'll be known to you as Gene Autry."

"Howdy, y'all," Gene said.

"Before we go any further," Boots said, "let's take a moment to honor Richard Willits, our Hopalong Cassidy. While you didn't get to meet him, he was an honorable man and paid his debts on time. Let us share a moment of silence in his memory."

People bowed their heads. I tilted mine but kept my eyes open and scanned the room to see if anyone else wasn't fully paying tribute to our honorable castmate who paid his debts on time. What had that been about? And who didn't pay their debts on time? Was Hopalong's death a way of paying his debt? If so, would others have their IOUs collected?

I bowed my head in time to hear Boots say, "May he rest in peace."

He paused a moment and then said, "I have to tell you that once word got out there'd be a Cowboy Poetry Gathering, it's been like lightning in a storm."

"You mean someone's gonna be here aside from us?" asked Gene.

"Yes, indeedy. If someone had said last year that they were going to have a poetry gathering, you and I would have been the only ones there, and I'm not certain about you. But call it *cowboy* poetry and it's magic. We got people coming here from the East Coast. There are magazines and newspapers here that some of you actually read. This is big time, people."

"Sounds like you hit pay dirt," said a well-heeled, tastefully dressed woman.

"Everyone, this here stylish cowgirl is Olivia Franz, who we'll be calling Annie Oakley."

"Howdy, everyone. Sorry I'm late, but what's that you say about hitting the big time?"

"I'm not here tooting my own horn. I'm here to tell you there'll be people in the audience listening to us. You're not professional actors, but you've all read your poetry or told your stories to somebody and this ain't too different than that. All you gotta do is read your part, look your part, and do your best to act your part. Plus, you all got your own reading and storytelling slot at the Gathering, so who knows what'll happen?"

I didn't want to say what I thought was going to happen.

"I want everyone showing up in the dining room each evening at six thirty so we can review the day's highlights. Other than that, and your own performance, the week is yours."

"The only time we need to be in costume is for the show?" Dale asked.

"Yes."

Wait. Costume? I didn't remember hearing anything regarding a costume. I'd been told to bring a costume to the mystery conference and had bought a Hercule Poirot outfit. I'd never been to Nudie's in North Hollywood but it would have been fun to go. Just about every cowboy and cowgirl in the movies owes their look to Nudie, and we in LA know that how you look is way more important than how you act.

"Some of us are already in costume," said Roy, who would have been if he were playing the earlier hands-on version of himself rather than the more stylish later one.

"Yes," said Boots. "I can see Annie, Buffalo, and Slick are in costume. But if the rest of you need brushing up, Capriola's will take care of you. It's a couple of blocks from here."

Evidently I was in costume. I was sporting the ad-exec-on-a-cowboy-vacation look. I'd have never said that about myself. Yes, I have a preppie look; I wear loafers, button-down shirts, and jeans. But Madison Avenue? Oh, well. At least I didn't have to worry about changing my outfit.

"I've had a change of plans," Boots said. "Which is the good thing about keeping the show loosely structured."

"You're going to take out Hopalong's part?" Duke asked.

"Someone took care of that," Gene said.

"The show will have to go on without him," said Boots. "But I've decided to slightly shift the focus. Initially, I wanted our show to focus on putting together the Gathering and the week's highlights. And while we were at it, we could poke fun at cowboy poetry. But now that Hopalong's been killed, we need to modify things. I still want us to have fun at the Gathering's expense, but I want us to go down a different trail."

"So tell us," said Duke.

"I'd intended to have Slick be a PR guy from Madison Avenue working with all of us cowboy poets on how to sell ourselves. I'd throw in some mischief to keep things interesting, but now ..."

"We're waiting," Duke said.

"Not all of you are as familiar with Slick as I am. Last year, I attended a mystery writers' conference in Vegas and we had to dress up as famous detectives. We were put into teams and had to solve a mystery. As you may have read, a bunch of people were murdered. If I hadn't seen it with my own eyes I wouldn't have believed it, but

Slick was able to get the killer to reveal themselves. He's a shrink and he used his highfalutin skills to solve that mystery."

I tried to not appear too highfalutin as people took a closer look at me.

"Since we've got a murder of our own, I'm going to ask Slick to take on a different role. We all know he ain't no cowboy, and even if he got himself all dressed up, he couldn't fool nobody coz he never fooled anybody in Vegas as that Frenchie detective."

"Belgian."

"Right. If we weave solving the mystery into the day's highlights, it's possible we'll be able to discover who killed our compadre."

"I'd be mighty proud to do that," said Duke, trying to sound like Duke.

"What has this got to do with Slick's new role?" Dale asked.

"That's tricky. On the face of it, I don't want his role to be any different. But I want him to help us find out who killed Hopalong."

That garnered me more looks, none of which appeared to be demonstrating any degree of assurance or reassurance. If I was going to help the group solve whodunit, it wasn't going to be on account of any investigative powers they'd invested in me.

"I gotta tell you," Boots continued, "I ain't no playwright. I'm not going to write us any dialogue. I'm just going to write out the highlights we discuss each day. Later, I'll pick who tells what story come Friday night. I'll give you each a list of the highlights and who'll recap each one with your own twist. It's storytelling, and I know you know how to do that. It doesn't take an idiot to see how this thing could go south real quick, so I'm counting on your poetic prowess."

"This is going to go to hell in a handbasket quicker than a fly to the outhouse," Buffalo said.

CHAPTER EIGHT

COMPANY FOR BREAKFAST

Monday January 28, 1985

NORMALLY I SHY away from sausages, pancakes, scrambled eggs, and toast, but when in Elko … I read the newspaper in the morning, but the local paper had yet to make it to the hotel. Before leaving LA, I'd had to make a choice—get a western from the local bookstore or wait till I got to the conference and buy a book of cowboy poetry. I chose Louis L'Amour's *The Riders of High Rock*, figuring I'd be getting more than my share of poetry during the week. As I ate my breakfast, I discovered I hadn't chosen well.

Fanciers of cowboy or cowgirl fiction might have the answer to this pop quiz. Given we're in Nevada, I'm taking bets. Want to place yours on who's the hero of *The Riders of High Rock*? If you said our newly departed cast member, you'd be correct. In the book, Hopalong was alive and well, and setting out to aid an old friend. Reading that was weird.

I PUT IT down when Cat asked if she could join me. Things were picking up.

"Please. How are you this morning?"

"I'm good. I slept well and I'm eager to go listen to today's presenters. How about you?"

"Yes to the week. No on the sleep. Whoever's in the room next door shared the highlights of their evening so I was a part and yet not enough of a part of it."

"You always talk like that?"

"Yes. No. I was trying to impress you and polished up my wordsmithing."

"You may want to rein it in. I might be a cowgirl poet but I spend a lot of time out on the range, where we tend to keep things a mite simpler."

"That makes things easier. What do you do on the range and where do you do it?" I said, trying to keep it simple.

"I'm from Missoula, Montana. My family owns a ranch."

"I've heard of Missoula. One of my favorite authors lives there— James Crumley. Do you know him?"

"No, I don't. Why's he a favorite?"

"His stories are exaggerated but his characters ring true to me. I was told he bases them on people he's met. Heck, it could even be someone in your family."

"I doubt that. We're not a very exaggerated family."

I wasn't making any inroads into getting her to like me. As for me liking her, swooning over her arresting looks had thrown me off base. She wore her long dark hair in a ponytail that showed off her high cheekbones, hazel eyes, and warm smile. While I didn't picture her as a librarian, I had a hunch when she took that band out of her hair and shook it loose, watch out.

"That's probably a good thing. Do you really spend a lot of time riding out on the range?"

"Of course. That's the high point."

"How so?"

"Ask anyone here and they'll tell you the same thing. That's where the poetry is. Out there in the expanse, it's a spiritual place."

"I'll grant you I was over-the-top with my wordsmithing but that's a pretty profound statement."

"Profound is usually simple. It's the word-spinning that takes you away from the truth. You'll see this week. Cowboys are simple, often humorous, and, like your Mr. Crumley, authentic but not exaggerated."

"You should be the PR person. You got me motivated to go."

"All right."

"What's all right?" Gene asked.

He was friendlier today, likely on account of Cat. He smiled at her and sat down beside her without asking.

I don't want to admit this, but it's the truth: I wasn't liking Gene. For no other reason than he was flirting with Cat. Not my finest quality but perhaps you can relate.

"I was telling Slick about the beauty of being on the range."

"She's a bountiful mistress."

Had that earned him points? It was poetic and simple, but in the city, we'd call it sexist. Humanist that I am, I kept quiet and let him self-destruct.

"Where do you hail from, Gene?" Cat asked. "I can't place your accent."

"Originally from the Panhandle, but more recently I've been holed up in Arizona cuz they still got wide-open spaces."

"That's one of the things I notice when I drive anywhere," I said. "You get outside the city and all of a sudden you have wide-open spaces."

"Yes, sir," he said to me.

Was he being deferential or calling me an old man? I was in the midst of being thirty-seven, and while I could hear forty calling, I wasn't fretting about it yet. I had at least ten years on him, but if he kept riding bulls, I'd have better long-term prospects.

"I saw you at the Stampede Rodeo last year. You were the star of the show," said Cat. I checked out the rest of the room to see if there were any other alluring women. It's not hard to tell when someone's starstruck.

"That was an ace-high day. I remember it well. If I'd seen you there, I'd have remembered it a whole different way."

That brunette in the corner was kind of interesting.

"You did see me there. You forgot. You were drunk."

Things were improving.

"I ain't never been that drunk. You sure it was me and not some other good-looking bulldogger?"

"It was you. You were with Bronco Shelton and a bunch of your rough-stock buddies. I was with people from the ranch. We shared a glance and then you turned away."

"Well, I ain't turning away now."

I didn't need to witness their carrying-on, and they were going to be carrying on. I took a last bite of sausage, gulped some coffee, and said, "See you both later."

CHAPTER NINE

MORNING ACTIVITIES

DOES EVERY TOWN in the middle of nowhere with ten thousand people have a convention center? I suppose so if they've also got legalized gambling, whorehouses, and a gold rush to offer.

Otherwise, why would anyone come? Weapons testing and poison-gas experiments aren't usually a big lure.

I had options. I could sit in on poets/storytellers at the Gathering doing their thing, go over to the museum and see the cowboy illustrations, view contemporary cowboy art in the Northern Nevada Community College Library, or stay in my room and read *The Riders of High Rock*.

I opted for the Gathering.

I like nature. We have some in LA. Anytime I take a walk outside, be it in a forest or a city, it's a nature walk. Nature enthusiasts may grimace but you take what you can get.

The temperature was predicted to reach thirty-two, so I wasted no time striding the mile and a half to the convention center. It was kind of invigorating. Living in LA, I'd forgotten what it was like to be out in freezing conditions. Coming back, I'd take a cab. There were scattered stores along the way, some basic one-story houses, and a high school that would have been at home in count-less other cities.

As I got closer, things picked up. There was a park with a base-ball field. Then the convention center materialized. It wasn't going to win any architectural awards unless it was a big year for nonde-script, but it would have central heating.

A couple hundred people were filling the lobby area. The first readings were due to take place at ten. I had three to choose from, one of which was someone called Clay Wilson. How many people called Clay do you know?

It was Buffalo. I'm not qualified to recognize a skillful poet, but I know what I like. I didn't think much of him as a poet, but he was a skillful bullshitter. He told stories about the cowboy way of life that, if they were true, clarified why the cowboy way of life hasn't thrived.

One story was disturbing, creative, and telling. He dragged it out, which I know something about. When he was out on the range for an extended period of time, he'd get very hungry and tired. He'd find a stream or a river and throw a stick of dynamite in it. Dead fish would float to the top. Supper.

I'm not someone who spends undue time at the market or in the kitchen prepping a meal, but I do care about the environment and the sanctity of life. I could see the time-saving value in his approach but couldn't endorse it. It did tell me overkill wasn't a big concern for him. If we did have more murders during the week he'd certainly be a suspect. As long as he didn't end up floating in the river.

When he finished a few people came up to speak with him, but instead of soaking up the adoration, he brushed them off. He was in a hurry to leave.

Not being in a hurry to do anything, I followed him.

He hustled to the parking lot. Where was Lucky when I needed him?

A couple of cabs were parked by the entrance. I'm a creature of habit, yet I don't like being totally predictable. Yes, I could have gotten into a cab and said, "Follow that car." I like saying that. But instead I said, "Hi there. There's a rusty old formerly blue Chevy pickup driving out of the lot. Can you follow him?"

"You bet," the cabbie said.

"Great. Thanks. Don't follow too close. I don't want him to know we're following him."

"You Lucky's friend?"

"What?"

"Lucky. You know, the cabbie you met in Vegas who saved your butt in Vero."

"Yeah. I know that Lucky. How do you know him?"

"I don't."

"Wait, you don't know Lucky but you know I'm his friend? Can you explain that?"

"He called up the office where I work and asked to talk to a cabbie. He got me. He told me all about you. He said you'd need a ride and some favors and to make sure I charged you plenty, cos you're a piece of work."

"That's very considerate of him."

"I'm only going to charge you what's on the meter. Well, until the funny stuff hits the fan."

"That's even more considerate of you."

"My pleasure. Want to tell me what we're doing?"

"As Lucky may have told you, I follow one thing until it leads to another. This guy could be going back to his hotel to take a crap or he could be going someplace else. All I know is he wanted to get out of the convention center fast and I didn't have anything to do, so here we are."

"I can tell you he ain't going back to the hotel."

"Well then let's see what he's up to. Since there's a chance we'll be spending more time together this week, what's your name?"

"Gus."

"So, Gus, want to tell me how you ended up being a cabbie in Elko?"

"Lucky told me to watch out for you as you're a shrink. Shall I just admit it was my mom's fault and we'll leave it at that?"

"It does cut out the foreplay."

"Aside from running away from her, I had enough of city living. I moved here ten years ago from Chicago. It's quiet, easy, and people leave you alone."

"I'm happy to leave you alone, but where's he going?"

"Gold country."

"I heard there was a bit of a gold rush. What's the story?"

"It's boom or bust here. Last couple of years, the population's been growing as would-be prospectors come in, trying to make their fortune. It doesn't happen, but while they're here, businesses make money and the schools get flooded. Then when their dreams come crashing down, they go back home."

"In the meantime, it's good for your business."

"If making more money means it's good, yeah, I'm making more. Not that I'd expect you to understand, but I came here for the quality of life. These dickheads, pardon the expression, are ruining it."

Not wanting to ruin it any more, I kept quiet.

The highway wasn't that busy so we followed a quarter of a mile behind until Buffalo turned off.

"What'll it be, boss?"

"We can't follow him down that road without him knowing. Slow down and as soon as he goes behind that bend, you can follow him."

"Whatever you say, but I gotta warn you."

"Yes?"

"Two things. Betsy here—that's the name of the car—don't take kindly to these dirt roads. We'll be needing some of those add-ons."

"Yes, and ...?"

"These roads twist all over the hills. He could be going a quarter of a mile or miles. I got the gas but I don't know if Betsy's got the guts. If you want to be stealthy about this, before we get to that bend, you're gonna have to get out, run up ahead, and peek. If you give me the all-clear, I'll come pick you up. But you don't want us bumping into him."

"Makes sense. I miss Lucky but I can tell you have your own skills. As for Betsy, what's it going to take for her to enjoy the ride?"

"Five bucks a mile."

"Betsy has expensive tastes."

"Just because we live in a small town don't mean we're stupid."

"No, you're not stupid. But what more am I going to learn by following him?"

"That's the question. What's the answer?"

"We won't know until we do. Hopefully, I'm only into Betsy for five."

Turned out to be ten. There were too many twists and turns that had me running up ahead only to wave Gus and Betsy forward. I was getting complacent about the peeking when I caught sight of Buffalo's Chevy pickup.

I signaled for Gus to turn the cab around in case we needed to make a hasty retreat.

Next to Buffalo's Chevy was an old Jeep and an entrance to a mine. I wanted to get closer but I'd be too exposed, so I watched for a bit, listened to the quiet, then rejoined Gus and Betsy.

As we drove back to town, Gus said, "Want to share? Isn't that what you shrinks say?"

"It is. There was a dusty Jeep there. I couldn't see anyone. There was an entrance to a mine. It even had an old sign, or part of one— F-o-o-t-s-t or something like that. I couldn't clearly make it all out."

"That's nice. A mine with a name."

"I'm not sure it was worth twenty to find out, but we'll see."

"Twenty to Betsy. You still gotta pay my fare."

"Thanks for reminding me. While we're at it, give me your card so I can get hold of you if need be. Do you have a beeper?"

"Does this look like beeper territory to you?"

"Not so much. Let me have your card."

"Lucky said to tell you to hire me for the week and make things simple," he said with a shrug.

"I do prefer to keep things simple. Especially as I have a knack for making things complicated. But I have my own car here—which I didn't want to use in Vegas, or have with me in Vero—so I'm not certain what kind of extra assistance I'll need."

"Lucky told me to offer you a weekly flat fee and a daily price. I can give you a break on the week. How about two fifty? It's that or a hundred a day."

"Does that include Betsy?"

"Betsy will charge her standard fee for out-of-town excursions."

"That's very consistent of her. I'll go with the daily plan, but it's comforting to know you're close by if I need you."

"Your call. Lucky also said to charge you extra for any stakeouts and shootings."

"What exactly does flat fee mean to you?"

Gus and I spent the rest of the drive ironing out the details.

CHAPTER TEN

LUNCH

I ASKED GUS to take me to his favorite place for lunch. He said his favorite place was on his couch, watching football. He dropped me off at the Giddy Up.

I vacillate between eating healthy and not. I also try to limit the number of dead animals on my plate because I know that, on a lot of levels, it's not good. If I was out on the range, overseeing a herd of cattle, I might feel differently, but I don't know which direction that would push me. People who live on farms raise animals and are able to kill and eat them. If they can do that, I can let go of judging them.

I opted for a salad. I was working my way through it when Duke and Lone came in. They were wearing mandatory cowboy gear—suede jackets, plaid shirts, jeans, boots, and hats. Cold weather was nothing new to them. I'd taken off my gloves, scarf, and peacoat and was down to loafers, jeans, T-shirt, and a wool sweater.

"Gentlemen, how was your morning?" I asked.

"Buffalo sure knows how to sling it," said Lone, picking up a menu.

"Please help me out. I know cowboys primarily from TV, was that fishing-dynamite story BS, or is that common practice?"

"I wouldn't call it common practice," Lone said. "I've never done that, but I've heard stories. What about you, Duke? Was Buffalo stretching the truth a bit?"

"I don't know Buffalo, but I wouldn't put it past him. He knows how to spin a yarn. No BS there."

"He didn't recite any poetry," I said. "Not that his stories weren't poetic, but what makes for a cowboy poet?"

Lone took a moment. "That's an interesting question. If you'd asked me last year, I'd have told you I had no clue. Still don't know much. You want to know how the term cowboy poetry and the gathering came to be?"

"Did it involve alcohol?"

"Could be. I wasn't there when they came up with it, but Duke was."

"Everyone gives Hal Cannon the bulk of credit," Duke said, peering up from his menu. "And he deserves it, though he'll tell Jim Griffith had the original idea. A group of us get together now and then. One time we were complaining about how poets never get their due. People go listen to authors give speeches, they go see plays, movies and concerts, but when was the last time anyone suggested you go take in some poets? You don't have to answer that—we all know the answer. Never."

"I can't ever recall seeing in the paper that a poet was coming to town."

"You're darn tootin'. I can't remember who said what, but by the time we were weaving our way home, we had the makings. Hal and a group of others have put barrels of elbow grease into bringing this about."

"So are you two poets or storytellers?"

"All of us are a bit of both, though none of us ever called ourselves a poet," said Lone, eyeing the waitress. "I lean more toward the poet side and Duke here's more of a storyteller."

"How about telling me a story? Want to tell me why Hopalong died? Is there a story there?"

"There's always a story," said Lone. "But not always one that can be told."

"Hold on. Are you saying you know why he was killed but you can't talk about it?"

"The more interesting story is who."

"That's why it's whodunit, not whydunit," I said, trying to sound knowledgeable. "Want to help me get on level ground and tell me why?"

"You'd be better served by asking Boots," Duke said, signaling the waitress to come and take their orders.

"I can do that, but why would I be better served with him?"

"You're kind of annoying, aren't you?" Lone said.

"That's not an uncommon observation. I prefer to regard myself as curious, but if I've overstepped a boundary, please tell me."

"One thing you need to know about cowboys and poets," Lone said, "is they ain't the most direct people."

"I'm starting to get that. And I know I'm the obnoxious big-city guy who's too nosey."

"We're getting that," they chorused.

CHAPTER ELEVEN

AFTER-LUNCH POETRY

I READ OVER the three scheduled presentations and opted for Gail Gardner. I wanted to listen to Annie, Dale, and Cat—well, mostly Cat—but wanted to hear some other women as well.

I sat down and listened. Turned out Gail had something in common with Johnny Cash, who wrote a song about a boy named Sue. Gail was also a boy, but not named Sue. You'd think I'd have learned more about making assumptions.

His poems were stories in rhyme. Some held universal truths; others eluded me. One was about two cowboys who run into the devil. He wants to take their souls but they lasso him, tie him up, and leave him where they found him. They manage to get home with their souls intact. Safe at home at night with your soul intact is as good a place as any to end the night.

The thing about the devil is, just because you've tied him up doesn't necessarily mean he'll stay that way.

When Gail was done, I loitered in the lobby people-watching. The majority were living the western lifestyle. I'm easily distracted when I spot an attractive woman, see animated gestures, or hear loud voices. All those things were taking place in various parts of the room, but I focused on the first.

"Hey, Slick, how you doing?" said Annie. Cat was by her side.

"I'm enjoying myself. I was listening to Gail Gardner relate an incident of tying up the devil. Is that a thing with cowboy poetry?"

"We cowboys know about the devil," Cat said, and in a way that made me want to know about him too.

"Really. How so?"

"I'll tell you how," Annie said. "When you're all alone on the prairie at night, there's a whistle in the wind that howls. The devil's out there waiting for you and soon may be coming to get you."

"I've heard that whistle in the city too," I said.

"I bet you have," said Cat. "But those of us who live in the wide-open spaces have a different connection to the devil than you city folk. When you're packed in that way, you have to keep a closer eye on those near you. We look more toward the horizon."

"That makes sense. I don't get to see the horizon very often. I hear it's nice."

"It's not about nice," Annie said. "It's more that we live closer to the earth. We deal with life and death every day."

"Yeah. I was daydreaming along those lines earlier. If you live on a farm or ranch, there are times you need to kill animals you've raised. That'd be tough for me."

"You learn," said Cat.

"I'm sure. You planning on learning anything special this afternoon? Any items of interest on the schedule?"

"I expect there'll be some goings-on tonight at the hoedown," said Annie. "You have anything on your plate for this afternoon, Cat?"

"I have errands to run in town and I ought to get going. I'll see you both later."

Phooey. That left me with Annie. Not that being with her was unpleasant. It just wasn't my first choice.

For someone who's supposed to be sensitive to the feelings of others, I can be insensitive. I'd talk to Annie for a little while before I wormed my way out.

"Tell me about yourself."

"What would you like to know?"

I imagined she wanted me to ask if she was single, but I wasn't that interested.

"Where are you from? What do you do when you're not hearing the devil whispering? And what's he or she saying?"

"I'm from Carson City."

"Where's that?"

"It's about 300 miles from here. Close to Tahoe."

"What do you do there? You a cowgirl?"

"I'm more a horse woman."

"What does a horse woman do?"

"I do what I please."

"That must be nice. What pleases you these days?"

"I like to volunteer."

As evidenced by her short responses, she wasn't liking this conversation—nor was I. If she did what she pleased and volunteered, did that mean she had ample money not to work? She wasn't flaunting any objects of wealth.

"That's admirable of you. What kind of volunteer work do you do?"

"I assisted with this event."

"You've done an admirable job. How about giving me some inside information."

"Such as?"

"Such as why Hopalong was killed. Did it have anything to do with this event?"

"Not that I'm aware of. But ask Boots."

"Somebody else told me the same thing. What am I missing?"

"Ask Boots. He can tell you. Now, please excuse me."

CHAPTER TWELVE

PARKING LOT

I DIDN'T FEEL like being indoors; although the last time I'd been outdoors, I hadn't felt like being there. Moments like these, I occasionally resort to my lesser life skills. Our dinner meeting wasn't for three hours, which gave me time to smoke a joint.

I made my way to the side of the building. I wasn't alone. Most people were smoking cigarettes—not one of my vices—but I smelled dope and headed toward it. If I'm going to be naughty, it's reassuring when others are joining in. In this case, it was Duke. He was staring out at the mountains, perchance dreaming about the gold hiding out there.

"Okay if I join you?" I asked.

"It's a free world," he said, and handed me the joint.

I tend to be cautious as you never quite know what you're getting into. I took a hit. Held it. Let it out. Then started coughing.

"Good shit, huh? Should have warned you. This is Prairie Gold."

"Never heard of it."

"I grow it myself."

"It's potent. I took a little hit and I'm lightheaded."

"Yeah. It'll shift your focus all right."

"Before I get too out of focus, I noticed you eyeing the mountains. Were you wondering if there's gold in them thar hills?"

"I wasn't wondering. Everyone knows there is. Lots of Cadillacs came out of those hills."

"I guess it comes down to where those Cadillacs are parked."

"Where they are and how you get them out without being ambushed. This is still the Wild West. Especially when there's a gold rush. It doesn't attract your best element."

"Thanks for the heads-up. Speaking of which, Lone said he had a notion why Hopalong was killed. Do you?"

"Possibly."

"How about sharing?"

"The answer is out there."

"Gold?"

"Could be. Ask Boots."

"Boots seems to be the holder of information. How do you know him?"

"We go back a long ways. We were in 'Nam together."

The Vietnam war was divisive. Many of those against it didn't think well of those who served in the military. I know because I was in the Navy at that time and got spat on when I was waiting for the subway in New York. I was out of uniform but my short hair was its own uniform. In 1985, the war was still a touchy issue. And while my naval service had qualified me for hate in the subway, it hadn't earned me recognition by those who'd actually fought. They were the real soldiers; the rest of us were something else. Duke didn't know my military background, so his sharing his information told me he wasn't afraid to stand up for himself.

"Thank you for serving," I said. "The people I served with hold a special place for me."

I was hoping I'd get away without having to identify how I served.

"Yep. When you go through shit together, you come out different than when you went in."

I could have regaled him with a story about a typhoon my shipmates and I had endured; but if he and Boots had gone through a firestorm together, better to keep that to myself.

"Come with me," Duke said.

He led the way to the parking lot and a dusty but impressive black Cadillac.

"Wow. This yours?"

"Yep, it's a '58 Coupe de Ville."

"You the original owner?"

"I wish. Got this a decade ago. Paid more for it than I did my first house."

"But your house didn't have fins."

"Not like these babies. Come on. Check it out."

I wasn't against seeing it up close and personal, but that's not what he wanted me to see.

He popped open the trunk. "Check it out."

The truck was big enough to stash multiple bodies if you were so inclined. Or a couple of oversized suitcases. He opened one with a key he'd pulled from his pocket.

I smelled it before I saw it.

"Prairie Gold?" I asked.

"You betcha. Hundred bucks a lid if you're interested."

"That's a bit more than I'm used to paying."

"Whatever they got out your way can't hold a candle to this. You know where I am if you're interested. But it'll all be gone by the end of the week."

"Hold on. First off, I'm happy to buy a lid so count me in on that. But you're confident you'll be able to unload all that this week?"

"Sure as eggs ain't chicken."

I wasn't entirely sure what that meant but was glad my order was in.

"Clearly, I don't know diddly about cowboys because I didn't know they smoked dope. I know they drink, but this?"

"Listen, sunshine," he said as he closed the trunk, "you surfers ain't the only ones who know how to have a good time. Most cowboys are drinkers, but I'm betting a couple of guys will pony up the bucks to take a suitcase back home with them and unload it at the other end."

"At a hundred bucks a pop it's going to be hard for them to make any money. That's more than people are used to spending."

"You buy a suitcase, I'll make it worth your while."

"Well, there's that. I'm not really a thief. More like a peeping Tom."

"You want to peek at the mother lode?"

"I want to see why so many people are going there."

"I'll tell you one thing."

"What's that?"

"This guy ain't going there."

"Yeah. Where's he going?"

"Hold your horses for a minute. I have, as you sleuths say, a suspicion. But, unlike others, I prefer not to assume things."

I wasn't sure if he'd meant for me to take it personally, but since I take everything personally, I did.

Gus slowed down. "You bring extra cash with you?"

"I've got some. Are we going gambling?"

"Of a sort. We're going for another mother lode."

"How so?"

"That guy is going to Mona's Ranch."

"There's a ranch in town?"

"This ain't that kind of ranch."

Buffalo parked outside a red building on the corner and Gus parked at the end of the block. We watched as Buffalo got out and strode into Mona's.

"So," I said, "is Mona's the kind of ranch guys go to when they've been out on the range too long?"

"There plenty of lonely cowboys round these parts. You fixin' on going in and investigating the mother lode?"

"Nah. But you need to go in."

"Me? Do I look lonely and horny to you?"

"I haven't looked that closely. I don't want you to go in to cure your blues. I want you to go in and tell them you're checking the place out and will be back later. And while you're there, see if you can see what our guy's doing."

"Want to tell me what our guy looks like?"

"The joint isn't going to be jumping."

"Lot of guys come over here for a nooner. It's convenient."

"He's in his late fifties, early sixties, heavy set. If he's still wearing his clothes, he'll be wearing a rumpled white hat, old Levi's, and a brown duster that's past its prime."

"I saw that from here, but that's half the guys in there."

"He uses moonshine for an after shave."

"Not sure I want to get that close to find out. Want to give me some cash so I can buy a drink?"

"I'll give you twenty dollars," I said, seeing his disappointment. "If you don't see him, ask where the bathroom is and see what you can see."

"Is this when we talk pay raise?"

"You can keep the change."

"Doc, Lucky said you weren't a cheapskate."

"That was nice of him. I'm buying you a drink for going into a whorehouse and checking it out. What kind of pay raise are you talking about?"

"Let's double-down on the twenty."

I handed him another twenty and made a mental note—I needed to add more cash to my gumshoe travel kit.

While I waited in the cab, my mind drifted back to Mimi's, the house of ill repute in Vegas where Louise oversaw the delivery of services. I imagined these establishments weren't networked but a call to Louise might be worth a shot. I wasn't anticipating much but long shots come in more frequently when a mystery is afoot.

Not too long after Gus entered, Buffalo left, hurried back to his car, and took off. Whatever the over and under is on time spent in whorehouses, Buffalo was coming in on the underside. And wherever he was going would be his own business as Gus appeared not to be in such a hurry. I considered commandeering the cab.

A couple of minutes later, Gus hustled his way down the block. "Sorry, Doc. We lost him, right?" he asked as he got behind the wheel. "I didn't want to be obvious and leave immediately after him."

"Yeah, I get that. If we can't catch up to him, we can go hunt for the mother lode elsewhere."

"Either way, we're welcome back there. I made the acquaintance of Sally, who told me they're having a cowboy poet special this week and to bring back all my friends."

"Well done. Did you see what our guy was doing? He wasn't there for the quickie nooner special."

"I shoulda asked about that. I told Sally that guys at the Gathering had been swapping stories about the place and I wanted to check it out. She said one of the guys from the Gathering had been in a couple of times and he'd just come in and was meeting with the boss. I asked to use the bathroom and went to see if anything was out of the ordinary, but nothing stood out. When I got back, Sally told me he'd left. But where did he go?"

CHAPTER THIRTY-ONE

LUNCH AND DESSERT

I WANTED TO go to the mine, but I get cranky when I miss meals so I asked Gus to take us somewhere for lunch.

"No problem. I've got the perfect place."

I can't conceive of describing a casino buffet as perfect, unless we were measuring in terms of gluttony.

The Commerce had a standout feature. I'd seen the oversized polar bear above the entrance as the casino was located next door to Stockmen's. What I hadn't seen was the ten-foot, four-inch version in the lobby—purportedly the largest polar bear in the world. What it was doing in Elko is anyone's guess. This wasn't exactly polar bear country. But there it stood in all its taxidermy splendor.

There's a basic philosophy when it comes to the buffet—make up for in quantity what you lack in quality. Holding true to that sentiment, I stuffed myself, just like the polar bear. By the time I pushed myself away from the table, I was as close to immobile as I wanted to get.

I wanted to nap on the drive to the mine, but that wasn't cricket as Gus likely wanted to as well. Instead, I elected to be a good team-mate and help him stay awake. Given his history, he might take his nap while I was in the mine. It was a risk. Still, he was all I had.

I needed Gus to keep a lookout on the other end of the string. A sharp tug from him would give me a warning, and one from me would tell him to come rescue me. I made sure to have him repeat that.

Our best-laid plans would have been laid to rest if there'd been any cars parked out front, but there weren't. I checked my flashlight again, then watched Gus tie the string to his arm.

The guy in the hardware store had said there was no average length for a mine. Could be miles or a few hundred feet. Gus got me a hundred yards; after that I was on my own.

I took off as many a miner before me had … hoping for the mother lode but facing bad air and probable disappointment.

I made it to my discarded pickaxe, stuffed it in my belt, and carried on. Soon I came to a ladder that descended into a hole. There are people who like heights and the dark; others, like me, prefer terra firma and the light of day. I inched forward and swung my flashlight down into the abyss.

"Nooo."

I turned off my flashlight, secured it in my pocket, and weighed a career change.

Is this how my clients felt when we worked together? A dicey descent into the unknown. The ladder was rickety and my loafers were wet. I inched my way down. And down. Questioning the necessity of doing this, but caught in my OCD need to finish what I start.

Desperate for respite from the dark, I took out my flashlight and held it with the kind of appreciation we reserve for those we love. I turned it on and glanced down. Big mistake. I couldn't see the bottom. I lifted my arm, ready to wedge the light back into my pocket, when the beam caught the edge of the shaft. The walls glittered. I peered closer. The only gold I'd ever seen was in jewelry. Was this the real thing, fool's gold, or what?

A tug on the string nearly caused me to slip. And, honestly, I was relieved. I didn't know what was going on at Gus's end but it couldn't be as precarious as what lay below me.

I pulled back to let Gus know I'd gotten his call and was on my way.

I tend to rush and I was quite keen to get out of that hole. But my loafers were still wet and the hole hadn't gotten any shallower so I took it slow and steady. Once I'd reached the top, I put down the pickaxe and trudged toward the entrance.

CHAPTER THIRTY-TWO

TUG OF WAR

I EXPERIENCED A mixture of emotions as I came out of the mine and into the light. Relief that I was out of that shaft and dread about what lay ahead.

Gus was there, awake, and much the same as I'd left him, aside from the dismay on his face. Standing next to him, in crisp clean uniforms, were two of Elko's finest. I'm not used to having police officers waiting for me, but when I've been pulled over I put on my best "How can I help you, Officer" face.

Gus beat me to the punch. "Doc, this is Sheriff Ralph Quinn and his deputy, John. I'm sorry, John, I can't remember your last name."

"It's Dough," he said, and Gus smirked.

"Officers, I'm glad you're here. I take it you're familiar with Gus."

"It's a small town," Sheriff Quinn said. He was tall, younger than John Dough, and had an unwelcoming glare on his drawn face. "Gus mighta told you we've had an increase in claim-jumping recently and received a report regarding unusual activity."

"Did Gus put your concerns to rest?"

"He tried, but we want to hear what you have to say."

"It's good you're here as I was hoping to speak with someone about the killings at the Gathering. I'm sure you're also on top of those. I'm part of the group that's lost some of its members and I've been asked to investigate."

"You a PI?" asked Deputy Dough.

"In my dreams. I've yet to find a name for what I do."

"You guys may not have heard of him," Gus said, "but this guy has a bit of a reputation for solving mysteries. He's a shrink but he's got skills."

That didn't earn me any accolades.

"What are you doing here?" the sheriff asked.

"Yesterday, I was out here with Duke. Sorry but I'm not aware of his given name. A group of us are in a show and we call each other by our character names. Duke was the guy who was shot in the park. Anyway, he said something that made me want to come back."

"What did he say?" Dough asked.

"It's what he did and didn't say. He was being obtuse but, like you, I'm used to that in my business. He said he was here checking on his investment. When I asked him if he owned the mine, he got evasive and told me he was checking on things but didn't want to do that while I was there."

I was being rather obtuse myself. I wanted them to assume I'd come here with Duke. My statement wouldn't exactly hold up to scrutiny so, like many criminals, I kept talking to cover it up.

"You may have seen the deed to the mine. That would certainly help clarify the matter as the murders are probably related to the mine. Although I'm not sure about Maverick. Do you know about Maverick?"

"The TV show?" asked Dough.

"Aw, sorry. I don't know his real name either. I suppose you've met with Boots. He knew Maverick. Who also got killed, but that was before the Gathering."

"We haven't heard anything about that," Dough said.

"You can follow up with Boots. He doesn't want the cast finding out as everyone might take off. But, if you count Maverick, we've lost Duke, the Lone Ranger, and Hopalong Cassidy. Sorry I'm not assisting you with those names, but Boots has all that information."

Whatever cachet I have as a solver of mysteries was lost on the officers; they were uncertain what to make of me. I hadn't even revealed my wiseass tendencies yet, so at least they didn't disrespect me. But they didn't respect me either.

"Want to tell us your whereabouts when Nathaniel Pierce, Duke to you, was killed?" asked the sheriff.

"I don't know when he was killed, but before we were told he'd been shot I was on a hayride. I didn't see him there, but he was at dinner with us."

"And after dinner?" the sheriff asked.

"I was in my room, tidying up, putting on a couple of sweaters and my jacket. Then I headed over to the hayride."

"It took you an hour to do that?" the deputy asked.

"I didn't have time before dinner. Plus I threw in a nap."

My alibi wasn't taking me off their radar.

"Sounds like you're a candidate for the last one to see him," said the deputy.

"Me and the rest of the cast at dinner. I didn't see anyone afterwards until we gathered for the hayride. For all I know, you were the last."

He didn't take kindly to that, yet I suspect that people who get into law enforcement are not unfamiliar with breaking laws.

No sense ruffling their feathers any more than I had.

"I'll tell you one thing that might be of interest."

"What's that?"

"If you're free tomorrow night, I suggest you swing by the Gathering for the closing activities."

"Because?" asked Dough.

"Not to witness my thespian talents. There'll be a show reviewing the week's highlights and the finale will include the big reveal. It's where we'll reveal who committed the murders."

"What?" asked the sheriff.

"This is where those sleuth skills Gus mentioned come into play. I'll spare you the long-winded answer."

They looked at me the way a lot of people look at me.

Then they did what a lot of people do when they meet me. They left.

CHAPTER THIRTY-THREE

PUSHING THE ENVELOPE

I MADE A phone call. Maybe Louise could help me sew together a couple of loose ends.

It was Thursday, five forty-five, which is happy hour most places, but early in a house of assignation. After a short wait she came on the line.

"Hey, Doc, how you doing? You in town? Want to play catch-up?"

"I wish. I'm still in Elko but have a reservation in Vegas Saturday so it'll be nice to catch up then."

"I'll pencil you in. Call me when I can ink it."

"Will do. If you help me out, it'll increase the odds."

"How's that?"

"Not surprisingly, people are getting killed and I've got more murders to solve."

"Doc, I may have to reconsider hanging out with you."

"Just don't go to a conference with me."

"It's not something I've been pining for," she said with a little chuckle.

"So, no worries. I don't imagine you're connected to similar establishments but there's a place up here called Mona's Ranch."

"Doc, I am connected, and we certainly get those Elko cowboys down here, but I'm not familiar with Mona's."

"That's too bad. Hopefully they'll extend you some professional courtesy."

"You said you were coming down here Saturday. You can't wait? You know I can take good care of you."

"Louise, if you and I ever get to the place where you take care of me, I know you'll take more than good care of me. But that's not the kind of care I'm wanting up here."

"That makes sense. If you're not wanting it from me, I'm not sure what you're wanting."

"Let's discuss that Saturday. In the meantime, can you call Mona's? There's a rough-and-tumble cowboy here called Buffalo whose name is Clay Wilson. He dropped by Mona's yesterday and has been in more than once. I want to know what he was up to. He wasn't there for a nooner as he was in and out faster than I'd want to be."

"Doc, if I wanted, I could get you in, off, and out before you could hold your horses."

"No one up here is in your league. Besides, he was up to a different kind of mischief."

"Give me your number and I'll call you if I learn anything."

"I'll give you my beeper number. I'm on a tight schedule here."

CHAPTER THIRTY-FOUR

STAR TIME

THE STAR WAS around the corner from Stockmen's. Boots had told us to arrive before six because there'd be a surprise. It wasn't hard to locate the place; it was a red building with a large red star on top. Boots said it was the best Basque restaurant in town. My expectations weren't high. If the décor was any indicator, they wouldn't be elevating any time soon.

At least there were no absentees. Boots sat at the head of the rectangular table. Dale, Roy, Annie, and Buffalo took one side. Gene, Cat, and I were on the other. We were surrounded by brown. Brown walls, brown wood, brown furniture.

As was his custom, Boots began by asking for our highlights. Gene shared how he'd spent the afternoon fishing in the Humboldt River. He'd taken his catch into the kitchen and they'd cook it up for anyone who wanted it.

While we all were reviewing the menu options, a bell rang. It wasn't a fire alarm and nobody was moving, but then a half-dozen guys filed in. This was Boots's big surprise. He explained they were boarders who, every night when the bell rang, would come downstairs and eat. Like Pavlov's dogs. He got a bigger kick out of that than the rest of us.

When we'd exhausted the highlight-sharing, I made my move.

"I ran into the sheriff today. It wasn't a highlight, but it got me thinking. We've lost members of our group, and we're at risk of losing more. While the sheriff is working to solve this from the outside, the answer lies within us."

"What do you mean?" asked Annie.

"I mean that there must be a connection between us aside from the show. That's what's putting us at risk. If we can determine that connection, we can work out whodunit."

Boots wasn't pleased with me. He'd asked me to solve this mystery but didn't want me ruffling feathers and wouldn't tell me what I needed to know. I didn't want to put pressure on him but I needed to get the ball rolling.

"How does this sound?" I said. "We each take a turn and share why we're here and our gut instinct about what's the connection."

"I'll go first," said Annie.

There's an Annie in every group. Just as there's someone who'd rather go last.

"I've known Boots forever. We used to be an item and we're still friends. He called me up back in the fall and asked if I wanted to help him out with this project. I jumped at the chance. The connection, aside from Boots, is our love of the West and the stories and values we carry forward."

"We were honored to come when he called us," Roy said. "We've known each other since high school. Dale and I have lived on a ranch all our lives, and while we can't sing as well as our TV counterparts, we can spin a yarn."

"Boots is a rambling man," said Gene. "We met up at a rodeo. It was in Amarillo but it mighta been Midland. That was a few years ago, but we run into each other now and then. When we ran into each other in Tucson three or four months ago, he invited me and here I am."

"You told me you met up in Grand Junction," Annie said.

"Well, we met there as well."

We all knew there was more to that story than Gene was telling, so I pushed.

"Want to tell us the rest of that story?"

"Boots and I worked together for a bit in Grand Junction. Neither of us want to remember how we got there or what we were doing there."

"And?"

"You want to answer that, Boots?"

"As Gene told you, it wasn't a high point in our lives, but you do what you can to get by. We were working for an outfit selling door to door."

"You never told me that," Annie said. "What were you selling?"

"Gene?" Boots said.

"Bibles and lava lamps."

"No way," said Annie.

"Yup, that's what we did," Gene said. "If people didn't want one, we'd sell them the other. We cleaned up pretty well before we had to leave town."

There were murmurs of interest.

"Boots?" Gene said.

"When you sell door to door, you run into lonely people who are thankful for the company. That's usually a perk of the job. Until the husband comes home."

No wonder Boots kept on the go.

There was an awkward silence while Cat and Buffalo wrestled over who'd go next.

"I'll go," Buffalo said. "Boots and I have a complicated relationship. Do you want to tell 'em, Boots, or should I?"

"Be my guest."

"This also took place years ago. Boots and I were in Pocatello and for a while I was his parole officer. That about it, Boots?"

"Sure," Boots mumbled.

Wait, wait, wait. I wanted to hear the rest of that story but it wasn't my place to ask. Fortunately, I wasn't the only curious one.

"Come on, Boots, tell us more," said Annie.

Boots was reluctant. How much of what he'd divulge would be the truth, the whole truth, and nothing but the truth?

"Gene said it; we did what we had to in order to make a few bucks and hit the road again. But I ended up broke in Pocatello and needed to put together some scratch. I've always been a gambler. And, well, I didn't make a smart bet."

I could tell he wanted to end the story there. But, heck, we all have our version of that song.

"So, come on," said Annie.

She may be a nuisance at times, but at that moment I was pleased she was on my team.

"I held up—well, tried to hold up—a liquor store and got popped. Did a little time and when I got out, Buffalo was my PO. We sort of struck up a bond and became friends. He helped me put this gig together."

Hmm. This gig? We'd all been told it was a show. While the sheriff or deputy might be dirty, I possibly picked the wrong arm of the law. A parole officer and a parolee could see eye-to-eye on some things. Not robbing a liquor store, but conceivably pulling some other scam.

Boots had the hustler in him. If he'd devised a plan for a score, who better to assist him than someone who'd spent part of their life shepherding convicts?

In some states, you'd get nothing more than a slap on the wrist for a first offense; jail time had to be earned. Perhaps the liquor store wasn't Boots's first rodeo.

"You're all excellent storytellers," Cat said. "That's why I wanted to go last ... see how you all told your stories. Based on that, I'd craft what I'd tell. So, here's my story. Boots and I met in a bar in

Missoula and he worked one summer at my family's ranch and we've stayed in touch. When he invited me, I said you bet."

Cat was crafting her story and being circumspect about it. Hadn't she said Boots and her family had an overlapping interest in jewelry? Lots of jewelry has gold in it. Cat never said what he'd been working on at the ranch.

"What's your story, Slick?" Annie said. "How do you know Boots and why are you here?"

I wasn't annoyed. It's good group practice if everyone shares.

"I haven't had the benefit of knowing Boots for a long time. Last summer, Boots and I attended a mystery writers' conference in Las Vegas. Sadly, people were murdered there. Fortunately, I was able to help uncover the killer. Even though we didn't meet at the conference, last week Boots was able to get a hold of me and asked if I'd help out here."

"I don't get it," said Annie. "Did you anticipate that someone was going to get killed? You invited the rest of us months ago."

Boots was distinctly uncomfortable. "I wanted Slick here just in case. He was an insurance policy."

"Not a very good one," Gene said.

"Why would you even think there'd be trouble?" Annie asked.

Boots signed deeply. "I invited someone else to be Maverick. Last week, he was killed for some unknown reason. I figured it was its own thing, but if trouble happened, I wanted Slick here."

"But why Slick?" Roy asked.

Boots took his time. I could have answered for him but was curious how he'd explain my presence.

"A couple of reasons. First, he's a shrink, and if we had any backstage conflicts he'd help us out. We're working well together so we haven't needed him."

He never spoken with me about that, but it was a fair assumption for him to have made. That said, he'd not mentioned my availability to anyone.

"And the second reason?" Roy asked.

"In Vegas, everyone was worried, naturally. And although the police were involved, it was Slick who psyched out what motivated the killer. If the murders of Maverick, Hopalong, Lone, and Duke are connected, let's see if Slick can forage his way through things and help the police apprehend the killer."

"What have you got, Slick?" asked Annie. "Whodunit?"

I had no idea. But one thing occurred to me. What had Boots been doing at a mystery writers' conference? Writing a mystery or getting tips on pulling off the perfect crime?

And, not for the first time, the more I knew, the less I knew.

"I don't know whodunit. I do know we can work together to solve this. As Boots said, I have experience helping groups work through conflicts. I suspect some of us are holding out, and it's hard to put two and two together when you don't have all the information. People don't want everybody knowing their business—it's not the cowboy way—but if everyone approaches me privately, I can try to put the pieces together."

I can tell when people are connecting with what I'm saying, and when they're not. This group's enthusiasm for my role, and for me, was in the trough.

"Listen," Boots said. "We need to work together to put an end to the killing and get out of this alive. Tomorrow, you'll each get your script in the morning so you can read through your part. We'll have dinner together and go over any last-minute plot changes."

"The show will go on," said Annie.

"Yes, it will," said Boots. "And, tonight, there's the poker tournament. So let's finish eating and then go over to the convention center and clean up."

I'd forgotten about the tournament. I've never been lucky in cards or in love. But if I played my cards right …

CHAPTER THIRTY-FIVE

THE POKER TOURNAMENT

PLAYING CARDS AND hanging out in saloons is part of cowboy lore. Any of the local casinos would have welcomed hosting the tournament, but they'd have wanted us to use real money. Instead, we were given a hundred dollars' worth of chips. When you lost all your chips, your night was over. We'd play in groups of nine. When tables got down to five players, others could join. There'd also be trophies for the winner and those accomplishing other feats.

I've never been into trophies, mostly because I haven't been involved in the kinds of activities that yielded them. However, I have a small but growing collection. I got my first one in college for a dubious achievement I'll save for another time. The second was from the mystery writers' conference after I solved the whodunit. And the third was for being on the winning baseball team at Vero.

Not being lucky at cards, I wasn't expecting to add to my total.

It was now or never. I haven't had any luck with conference romances and I've yet to write a decent sex scene. A woman in Vero pointed that out to me, and I explained that in order to write one, I'd need to have one. I wanted that to translate into an offer, but as with too many prospects, it fizzled out.

Cat had some interest in me. She'd also been impressed when Gene put a serious move on her, though I hadn't seen them canoodling or otherwise triggering my annoyance. The coast was as clear as it was going to get. Since she lived in Montana and I in California, neither one of us was betting on anything more than a conference romance, although part of me was kinda hoping for more.

I arrived at the tournament and found her sitting at a table with empty chairs. None were next to her, but I took a seat anyway.

The table filled up and we made small talk, which I prefer not to do but you do what you gotta do. We were given our chips and put in a three-dollar ante. The game was five-card draw. Everyone gets five cards. You bet. You can keep or discard as many as you want. You bet again. Winner takes all.

My card-playing days are mostly behind me. My parents taught me how to play gin rummy and bridge, and I played at home with them and my sister. In high school, I played bridge and poker with friends, but that was a long time ago.

We'd played three hands and I was down to eighty dollars, but I was feeling sanguine. I'd been dealt three jacks, a queen, and an eight. Here's where my card play could use some improvement. I needed to keep the jacks, but should I keep the queen or eight and hope to pair up? Eight is my lucky number. Then again, I could discard both and hope to land a jack or a pair. If I were a serious player, I'd have memorized the odds.

Someone put in five dollars. Someone else raised ten. Cat threw in fifteen and I joined her. I let go of my lucky eight and queen and was rewarded with a pair of kings. I tried to keep a poker face. The first guy put in ten dollars. The second guy raised him ten. It was twenty to Cat. She was hesitant. It was a fifth of our stake, but after taking a moment she was in. I tried to appear unsure as I matched the twenty dollars and then raised it fifteen.

I tried to shrug off the stares. It was the first big pot of the game and, like those old gunslingers on the street, we were facing off.

The first guy dropped out. The second guy saw my fifteen and bumped it ten. *What have I gotten myself into?*

Cat looked like she was feeling the same way. Throw good money after bad or hold out and hope the fates are with you? She matched my fifteen and the other guy's ten.

I checked my used-to-be pile. There was enough to match the ten dollars and have a little left over. What the hell. I'd either hit the jackpot or I wouldn't. I shoved my remaining chips into the middle of the table.

"All in."

The guy matched me. Cat glared at me as if I was crazy. Any respect and care she'd had vaporized. Reluctantly, she put her chips on the table.

As I was betting last, I assumed I'd get to show my hand last, but it turned out that the last person to make an aggressive bet goes first. I showed a modicum of restraint as I laid my cards out. Three jacks, two kings. The first guy swore under his breath and didn't bother to show his hand. I smiled at Cat, who shook her head and placed her cards down one at a time. A two, a four, a four, a four and a four. Four of a kind.

She wasn't overjoyed as she swept the chips in. I tried not to let my disappointment show as I said, "Well played."

I got up and sulked out of the room. One of the organizers standing by the door commiserated with me. It didn't go far. I heard the parental lectures. *David, don't get overly excited. Be patient. Don't rush.* I had a flashback to a sign I'd seen at the music festival—*The Beatings Will Continue Until Morale Improves.*

I slinked out to the lobby and took a moment to comfort myself. *It's only a game. Let it go.* I didn't make much headway. I was alone in the lobby. The rest of the losers would join me eventually.

My beeper vibrated. I found a pay phone.

"How you doing, cowboy?" Louise asked.

"Better now that I'm talking with you. I just lost all my money in a poker game."

"Then you don't need to stop by on your way home."

"Louise, I wasn't aware I was a paying customer."

"You haven't been, that's for sure. As for the future, we'll have to see."

"Yes we will. You got any news for me?"

"I had a chance to speak with the manager, Nina. She said she'd hook you up."

"That's good to hear but that isn't what I was looking for."

"She said—and I tend to agree—that's what they're all looking for."

"There's some truth in that, but what I was hoping to find out was what Buffalo Bill was doing there."

"She said he was a shareholder."

"A shareholder?"

"Yeah. You know. Someone who owns a share."

"You mean like an investor? Could I own a piece of your action?"

"Honey, that's not going to happen. But see what Nina has to say. Maybe you can buy in there."

"My evening's open. I'll go over and see what I can do."

CHAPTER THIRTY-SIX

SHAREHOLDERS

THE BORDELLO BUSINESS has to be risky. Yes, it's a time-honored service and I imagine the interest hasn't dwindled over the years. Why had Buffalo judged it to be a good investment? Stockholder meetings?

I checked in with the bartender at Mona's and she left to get Nina. The place wasn't as fancy as Louise's but it had its own—not charm per se—let's say appeal. There was a working fireplace in the corner and brick walls that helped keep everyone warm, especially if they were wearing lingerie. A woman who'd clearly logged in gymnastic classes slithered on a pole in the middle of the room. A few men sat on red faux-velvet sofas frequented by scantily clad women.

Louise had set the bar high but Nina had her own thing going. Whereas Louise was a solid six feet, Nina was closer to five-five, though the silver platform boots gave her a certain stature. She couldn't go toe-to-toe with Louise's synthetic enhancements, but made up for it with what nature had bequeathed. And like Louise, she didn't hesitate to show off her assets.

"You the guy Louise called about?"

"That's me. Thanks for taking the time to see me."

"Louise said you were a piece of work and I'd get a kick out of meeting you."

"Well, that's kind of her. She's a piece of work herself, as are you. Since we all have something in common, maybe you'll be able to help me out."

"She told me you're a PI, Clouseau type who fumbles around but has the smarts to be able to put things together. Is that it?"

"I'm not keen on the Clouseau part, but I've been able to help solve some murders. As I'm sure you're aware, we've had some at the Cowboy Poetry Gathering and I want to see what I can do."

"Come with me," she said, and sashayed down a hallway.

I'd been down a hallway with Louise and come to an office that was influenced by the Marquis de Sade. While Louise had a certain natural flair for mastery and submission, she'd held back from taking me to places I'd rather not go. I wasn't sure where Nina was taking me, but I was happy to follow.

She, too, had an office—a tidy desk, a couple of chairs, a sofa, and a bookcase filled with porn videos, but no torture chamber. I wanted to see if any of Dr. Goodst's or Trixie's videos had made the cut, but I was distracted by the large velvet paintings on the wall.

"Are they you?" I asked.

"They ain't your Aunt Esther."

"You'd be surprised, though she can't hold a candle to you."

"Have a seat," she said.

I took the sofa and she sat in one of the nearby chairs.

It was just as well I was facing the bookcase and not the pictures. But, then again, I had the real thing in front of me. Although she wasn't velvet.

"What can I do for you?"

One thing she could do would be to sit on my lap so I'd have a decent sex scene to write. But that was kinda off-topic. Plus, would I be disloyal to Louise? I hadn't slept with Louise, hadn't even kissed her, but she had tied me up and we were flirting. It also was disloyal to Maverick, Hopalong, Lone, Duke, and Cat. Not that they'd be dealing with their disappointment in the same way as Louise.

"Generally, do you have any insight into what's going on? Were you familiar with any of the dearly departed? Were they customers?"

"And specifically?"

"A sixty-year-old beat-up cowboy came in yesterday close to noon. He was here for a short time and then took off. His name is Clay Wilson. Evidently, he's been in and out this week but not for the physical attention. Do you know why and whether it relates to the murders? Louise said he was a shareholder."

"I get it. I want to help. Murders ain't good for business. This Gathering is the best thing for business we've ever had. I wish they'd do it again, but if people keep getting deep-sixed, others won't want to come."

"I'm with you. Hal Cannon is a good hand and if anyone can make this go forward, he can."

"I never heard of him."

"Yeah. I'm not surprised. He's got other interests now."

"There's always an interest," she said, slyly smiling at me.

"You flirting with me?"

"Haven't made up my mind."

"That shifts things a bit. Can you help me otherwise?"

"I'm privy to things that it wouldn't be wise for me to share. Louise said you were a shrink, so you know about keeping things private."

"I do, but there's a limit to confidentiality. If someone is a danger to themselves or others, I can legally break a confidence."

"That may be legally okay in your business, but in my business it ain't good for business."

"I'm sure. Let me show you a way you can slip by that and not worry. Therapists do it all the time. Let's have a hypothetical conversation. Say X came in here and did some business that wasn't business as usual. If Y knew, it could prevent Z from being hurt. What might Y do to find out what X was up to?"

"You are a piece of work. It kinda turns me on."

"Really? That's exciting. I'd prefer to skip the foreplay and jump your bones, but come on, help a fellow out. Can you share some of that privy stuff?"

She lifted her shoulders and shrugged, which caused her chest to rise and shudder.

Focus, David.

"Someone might be making a payment."

"They have a bill and they're coming in to pay it off?"

"We extend that courtesy to select people."

"That's very gracious of you. Is that the kind of courtesy someone dropping by at noon yesterday might have taken advantage of?"

"There are other payments to be made."

"Meaning people use you like a bank?"

"We're more a safe-deposit box. We have reliable police protection and people don't cause trouble here. Safer to rob the bank."

"I'll keep that in mind."

"You do that," she said, and sat down next to me on the couch.

"It's nice to have you come sit closer. You're a very attractive and alluring woman."

"Thank you," she said in a way that made me want to thank her more.

"Can you tell me hypothetically what kind of payments someone would want you to hold?"

She stood up.

I can have that effect on people.

"It's been a pleasure meeting you. Come back when you have other things on your mind. It's time for you to leave now."

"I'll certainly do that. But before I go, can you at least tell me what the payments are for?"

"Stand up and come here."

I did.

Her body brushed against mine as she whispered in my ear.

Then she opened the door and let me out.

I took my time getting back to my car. I've never "been" with a professional sex worker. Well, not in the United States, but we'll save the Navy stories for another time. Nina was attractive and seductive, and I'd been swept up in her. I wouldn't have minded spending more time with her, though no doubt my fear of all manner of transmittable diseases would have convinced me otherwise.

Nina hadn't whispered sweet nothings in my ear.

She'd said, "Gold."

There'd been gold in the picture before and here it was again. Buffalo had made a payment for what? A share in the mine? If so, why be so secretive? If I was selling shares, I'd be telling everyone they were for sale. And if I was buying in, I'd be telling my friends, who'd wish me luck and tell me I was crazy.

A car drove up the street and parked. Annie climbed out and hurried into Mona's. Minutes later she came out.

It was possible shares were for sale and I wasn't on the mailing list.

CHAPTER THIRTY-SEVEN

THEY SAY MORNING'S A GOOD TIME TO THINK

Friday February 1, 1985

IT WAS THE last full day of the Gathering. If I was going to solve this thing, it wasn't going to be by following a trail of clues until I caught the culprit. I didn't even know which trail to take or where to find it. What I could do was review the list of suspects and see if there was any insight to glean.

Boots had his own ne'er-do-well flim-flam past. He'd been at the mystery conference. He was trying his hand at theater production. Why?

Cat cleverly played her hand and fooled me. She had my romantic interests, but I wasn't feeling we were going anyplace. She'd crafted her story and avoided saying anything about jewelry.

Buffalo had made a payment on a gold mine. I'd seen him at the mine. He'd been Boots's parole officer. And he made moonshine, which wasn't exactly a highly regarded, law-abiding activity.

Gene was a rodeo cowboy who'd been up to no good with Boots and fancied Cat. That didn't qualify him as a killer, but I had the least sense of him. Was he purposefully keeping a low profile or I was purposefully avoiding him?

Annie. She'd made a payment too. The nosy, earnest one, a bridesmaid-never-the-bride type. Had the men who'd been killed left her behind?

Dale and Roy appeared to be the stereotypical wholesome albeit emotionally distant couple. What lurked behind their curtain?

Sheriff Quinn and Deputy Dough were long shots but would make for an unexpected twist.

Hal, Gus, Nina, Louise, me ... even longer shots, but they, too, come in now and then.

This wasn't getting me anywhere, though I'd seen a glimmer of what I had to do. It had no shape, form, or content. Just a spark.

I'd need to stir the brew and cook a killer. I'm not much of a chef so that metaphor isn't ideal, but it got me mulling.

A concoction of facts, leads, assumptions, and accusations could be blended to retain everyone's attention until the killer was thoroughly poached and revealed themselves. All I needed was the right recipe. I'd created these concoctions before, and used group pressure to get people to share what they otherwise wouldn't have.

If that doesn't sound plausible, then you've never been in group therapy. I have. And facilitated it. Groups are powerful things. Picture it this way: you're at home, reading a book, or taking a stroll and listening to one. It's unlikely that you'll suddenly start confessing your sins. But in a group where people are disclosing things they usually don't share, your emotions get tweaked and you're liable to behave differently. People confess all manner of things.

But murder, you ask? I admit it's a stretch. But for reasons beyond my full comprehension, I've been able to stir the pot such that pressure mounts, secrets slip out, and truths surface.

So how was I going to pull it off this time?

I went down to breakfast, then went out to break the law.

CHAPTER THIRTY-EIGHT

OFFICE VISIT

I DON'T INCLUDE myself as a member of the criminal fraternity, but if breaking laws qualifies me, I am. But, your honor, I'm guilty with an explanation.

I'd tried that line of defense in traffic court but it hadn't worked. I haven't been back to court and have no desire to, but if I were to stand before a judge, like most every other criminal, I'd put my crimes in a context that spoke of my greater innocence.

I headed over to Hal's office at the museum. As before, the museum was quiet. I meandered down the empty hallway to Hal's office and knocked. No answer. I took a quick breath, said, "In for a penny, in for a pound," and slipped in.

The last time, Buffalo had thrown me off my game, and I hadn't fully taken the place in. Hal's desk was well maintained if you didn't count the stacks of paper and files covering it. Because it was all new to me, I sat down and initiated a search, cognizant that although it seemed disorganized, Hal would notice if I put something back in the wrong place.

I trawled through letters, bills, flyers, and a postcard of someone on a bucking horse. I read it, even though there was no need, and discovered Julie wished Hal was there with her. I combed the letters and bills, hoping to find something that would make my breaking the law justifiable. The clock was ticking but I didn't want to leave empty-handed. I glanced at the bookcase—mostly shelved with artifacts that could easily have been in the museum proper. There was also a filing cabinet that I wasn't anxious to explore so I kept my sights on the desk.

I picked up a short letter thanking Hal for the opportunity. Not Julie this time. Printed on the letterhead was:

Boots Sarandon
Bootstrap Mine
Elko, Nevada

I'd gotten my clue. No need to be greedy, stay, and search for more. I was a free man and desired to remain so. I opened the door a crack, took a peek, and made my escape.

What was the opportunity Boots had been so grateful for? Did it have to do with putting on the show at the Gathering, or with the mine? And where did that leave Hal?

CHAPTER THIRTY-NINE

BACK AT THE CONFERENCE CENTER

WHILE I WAS feeling full of myself, others were less so. Heads were hanging, tones were hushed. No last-day merriment in evidence.

I slowly approached Roy, who was alone in a corner. "What's going on?"

"It's Annie. She's dead."

"No. That's horrible."

I had no words, just sorrow. We stood silently together. The cowboy way.

Then curiosity got a hold of me. The city way. "Was she shot too?"

"Yup, in her room. Last night. She never showed up for breakfast so Cat had the manager check on her. It keeps getting worse."

"Yeah. I'm the kiss of death."

He inched away.

"What I mean is, I go to a conference and people die. I go to a music festival and people die. I go to a baseball camp and people die. I'm not what you'd consider a good-luck charm."

"You need to stay home more."

"There is that. I don't mean any disrespect to Annie, but have you been to Mona's this week?"

"How do you know about that?"

"I have some skills and a fair share of luck."

"Not at cards."

"You heard?"

"If you'd not left with your tail between your legs, you'd have heard the winners being announced."

"Anyone in our group?"

"Our group didn't have any big winners, but you got yourself a trophy."

"What? I got a trophy?"

"Congratulations. They called it The First Losers Cup."

"Ouch. I felt lousy when I lost, so I'm not sorry I missed the final humiliation. That said, I have a small but ever-growing trophy case. I'll put that high up and at an angle so no one can read it."

"What kind of trophies have you got?"

"Let's save that topic for later. You wouldn't be interested. Why don't you tell me about your visit to Mona's?"

"Now I'm more interested in the collection."

"I'm sure you'd be fascinated by it, and someday, when we do some moonshine or the equivalent, I'll tell you. In the meantime …"

"I went, paid for my share, and that's that."

"Very nice. Your share of …"

"You're the sleuth. You figure it out."

"All right, play hard to get. But you could be next on the list. Unless you're the killer. If you are, throw me off track. And if you aren't, what's going on?"

"Somebody doesn't condone sharing."

"I found out Annie was an investor. Same for Hopalong and the Lone Ranger?"

"You're guess is as good as mine. I was told that no one's sure who's involved, but it's a finite number. You do the math. The fewer the investors, the larger the share."

"That makes sense, but doesn't that make it obvious? If you're the last one standing, where's the finger going to point?"

CHAPTER FORTY

WHY BE A SORE LOSER (ESPECIALLY IF YOU HAVE A TROPHY FOR YOUR EFFORTS)?

I WANTED TO comfort and console Cat. She'd grown close to Annie and would be hurting. The pain of death doesn't go away. People go through stages of mourning. The best you can do is to be with them when they want you to be and not be with them when they don't. The goal isn't to make them feel better but to be with them while they feel. That's easier to say than it is to do.

The lobby was crowded. Dale and Buffalo were talking with a group of people I didn't recognize. Gene was with some guys who looked like they made their living on the rodeo circuit. Boots was engaged in an animated discussion with Hal.

I finally saw her alone in the large meeting room.

Quietly I stepped over to her. "Okay if I join you?"

She nodded.

I sat down and remained quiet. Trying to be with her as best I could.

It wasn't long before she said, "This sucks."

"Big time."

"What did she do? She was the nicest person. It makes no sense."

If I'd been her therapist, I'd have encouraged her to share the anger and fear simmering below her words. But I'd been hired to find out whodunit. That meant blending my therapeutic and sleuthing skills, and one would need to take precedence.

"I don't get it either. Why kill her? Has it got anything to do with her share?"

"Her share?"

"You know. The one she was dealing with when she was over at Mona's."

She gave me a bewildered stare, turned away, and began to cry.

I wanted to be empathetic but I didn't believe her. Was she bluffing or did she really not know about the shares? Fool me twice, shame on me. I wasn't ready to call her bluff, and I wasn't ready to share in her sorrow. So I shut up and waited her out.

I ought to stop mentioning how therapists let clients break silences, but here I go again. I can't help it if that's what we're taught. And I can't help it if that's not what I practice. Well, I can and there are times I do. This time I gave it close to five minutes, which for me is a long time. In my younger days, I'd have maxed out at a minute.

"What's going on?" At least I'd focused on the moment at hand.

"I could have stopped it."

"You could have stopped it?" I said, getting solid As from my teachers for reflecting.

"Possibly. Annie was in trouble. We all are."

"You know what's going on and who's doing this? If so, I'm here to help. That is, if you want."

"I don't know. I wish I did."

"But you said you could have stopped this. What did you mean?"

She turned toward me, her eyes full of tears. If they were crocodile ones, she was putting on a good show. She studied my face—a not altogether unpleasant experience—as if searching for something within me. I wanted to have what she was looking for, but that would depend on what she was looking for.

I can handle eye contact and most of the time the other person leaves first. When I'm doing therapy, I don't want to leave them until they're ready. Outside of the office, I value the connectedness … until I become uncomfortable.

"I'm getting uneasy. Want to tell me what you could have stopped?"

She examined her hands.

"The greed. I should have stopped it in its tracks but I didn't. I have to go. Thanks for coming over. I'll be fine. I need some time to set things right."

CHAPTER FORTY-ONE

SET SOME THINGS RIGHT

CAT WANTED TO set some things right. I wanted to know what those things were. So I followed her. She rapidly made her way out the front entrance. I wondered why she hadn't mentioned my trophy-winning performance and her contribution to it. She did have other things calling her attention, and it's not always about me, but she had snookered me. If the tables were reversed I'd have rubbed it in. Maybe she was more grown-up than me.

She took off for the parking lot and hustled toward her car. I was on my way to my car when Gus pulled up alongside me. I opened the door.

"We back in action, Doc?"

"You bet. She's down that row. Let's see what she drives out in."

A black Jeep Cherokee.

There was a tap on the window. Deputy Dough. I rolled the glass down.

"Can I have a word with you?"

Not now is what I wanted to say. "My pleasure" is what I said. I got out and turned to Gus. "Why don't you go run that errand." In case he wasn't sure what I meant, I winked. Then I gave the officer my full attention. "Good morning, Deputy. How can I assist you?"

"The sheriff and I are speaking with all of the people who knew Olivia Franz, Annie Oakley to you."

"It's awful. From my experience with her, she wouldn't have hurt anyone."

"Plainly not everyone feels the same way."

Did he mean the killer or had he heard from others who'd expressed that sentiment?

"Can you tell me when you last saw her?"

Don't you hate questions that make you hesitant to tell the truth? I'd last seen Annie at Mona's. And while there was nothing wrong with my having seen her there, there wasn't a lot right about it either.

"Last night."

"Here at the convention center?"

"Yes, but someplace else too."

"Where was that?"

"I was parked outside Mona's Ranch. By your expression, I can tell you're familiar with the place. I was sitting in my car, deciding what to do, when she went in."

"She went into Mona's?"

"Women do, but she was in and out in under five minutes."

"What time was this?"

"I'm not positive. Nineish."

"Well, that makes you the last one who saw her. That seems to be a thing with you. What did you do after she left?"

"I drove back to the hotel."

"The same one she was staying in?"

"Yes, we're all staying there."

"Did you follow her immediately?"

"No, I stayed outside Mona's a while longer and then came back."

"Anyone see you after that?"

"I walked through the lobby and up to my room. I didn't talk to anyone."

"No witnesses?"

"Truthfully, I'd wanted to have company, but that didn't work out."

"Too bad. The sheriff wants you to swing by the station before you leave town."

"Will do," said the burgeoning suspect.

CHAPTER FORTY-TWO

CAN WE TALK?

I WASN'T LIKING the turn of events. While I'd had a hunch more murders were coming, I'd been leaning toward the targeting-men theory.

So why Annie? Whatever people were buying at Mona's, it wasn't life insurance. Had Annie been killed because one fewer shareholder meant more for the rest?

The small piece of the picture I saw suggested those investments were not as secret as some might wish. Someone was increasing their stake. If it was a company on the New York Stock Exchange, that would have meant hundreds of thousands of shares. But with Bootstrap Mine, the number would be considerably lower.

Was everyone in the cast except me a shareholder? Cat had indicated otherwise but she'd already fooled me once.

I needed someone who'd spill the beans. I wasn't counting on Boots being that person, but it was he who came up to me and said, "We're up shit creek. We need to talk."

"I'm with you on that. Where do you want to go?"

He hastened down a hallway, found an empty room and beck-oned me. I have to admit, I was apprehensive. Boots wouldn't invite me only to kill me, would he? But a week like the one we'd had puts you on edge. During my therapy training, I was taught if I was uncomfortable to sit between new clients and the door. That was advice worth following now.

Boots wasn't sitting, so I stood between him and the door.

"What's up?" I asked.

"Everyone's on my case and blaming me for Annie and the rest. If I'd wanted to kill all these people, I wouldn't have gone to the trouble of bringing them here."

"Why did you bring them here? It wasn't for the show, was it?"

"Yes it was."

"Here's why everyone's blaming you. You don't tell the truth. Now, granted, most of us hedge our bets, but you're not owning up to things you need to own up to. You can't expect people to trust you if you keep lying."

"Who says I'm lying? I'm not lying."

"Come on. You didn't hire me to be your shrink, so I'm not going to have a heart-to-heart with you, but even I can tell you're lying. Or misleading. Or avoiding the truth. You said you're not lying. That's a lie. If you can't own up to the easy ones, who's going to buy into the more difficult stuff?"

"Sometimes I exaggerate," he said as he sat in a chair.

"That's closer. You're a sales guy. But if you want me to solve this thing, you need to share deeper truths with me." I sat down while he took a moment.

"What do you want me to say?"

"I'm interested in the gold mine and people's investments."

"You know about that?"

"You asked me to look into things. Money and murder often go hand in hand. What kind of opportunities are there?"

"Opportunities?"

"Come on. You thanked Hal for the opportunity. For what? To put on the show? Sell shares?"

"You don't understand."

"There are lots of things I don't understand. Help me understand why people are being killed and what's going on. The good news is, I don't think you're the killer. You could be. But, as you said, why bring your victims here? Especially since you're a guy that doesn't mind traveling. So, come on, what aren't you telling me?"

"Slick, I've said this to you before," he said, looking me in the eye. "I can't."

"Can't or won't? There's a difference."

"Not to me."

"How about this? Don't tell me. Just nod your head when I say something you agree with and shake it side to side when you don't. Can you manage that?"

He nodded.

"Does this concern the gold mine you own?"

He nodded, then shook his head.

"Is this partly concerning the gold mine?"

He nodded.

"Do you own it?"

He nodded and shook his head.

"Did you own it and sell some shares?"

He nodded and shook his head.

"Recently?"

He shrugged.

"Did you sell shares to the dearly departed?"

He shrugged.

"The shrugging isn't helping."

He shrugged.

"Are the deaths connected to the shares?"

He shrugged.

"Just so I'm clear, are present and past members of the cast stockholders in the mine?"

He shrugged.

"Is Buffalo a shareholder?"

Nod.

"Gene?"

Shrug.

"Dale?"

Shrug.

"Roy?"

Shrug.

"Cat?"

Shrug.

"Any others outside our group?"

Shrug.

"Did I mention that shrugging isn't helpful?"

He nodded.

"Anything else useful you can tell me?"

He shook his head.

"That wasn't too bad. You didn't tell me a thing. We can both vouch for that. So don't tell me now, is someone blackmailing you?"

Small nod, a shake, and a shrug.

"And you can't tell me who."

Nod.

"And I take it you won't tell me why."

Nod.

"Anything you can tell me?"

"Figure this out before anyone else dies."

"That works for me. When we do our show I want to have the last speech. We'll all be lined up on the stage and write on everyone's script that I will give the final curtain speech. I have the beginnings an idea how we can get the killer to show his hand."

"You do?"

"Not a fully developed one—there's a couple more pieces I need to put together. If I can psych out why someone's killing these people, I can try to do some voodoo-therapy magic to get them to reveal themselves."

"Break a leg."

CHAPTER FORTY-THREE

BREAK A LEG

I ONCE HEARD it's not lucky to be superstitious. I get a kick out of things like that.

Now that showtime was approaching, it was time to break out the showbiz superstitions. I have a more than adequate number of my own superstitions not to need other people's. That said, I wanted my closing monologue to bring down the house.

I needed to uncover a motive. It could be greed or it could still be hiding.

I ought to touch base with everyone in the cast again. Plus, the longshots on the list: the sheriff, the deputy, and the madame.

I don't have to tell you where I went first.

The small bar was holding up three guys who were beyond caring about paying jacked-up prices for watered-down drinks.

It would be hard for me to work the morning shift and listen to Van Halen sing "Hot for Teacher" while one of the dancers tried to make a go of it on the pole. I asked the bartender if Nina was available, and after a verse she showed up. In bordellos and casinos time takes on a different meaning. There's only gambling time and get-it-on time.

Nina was still looking worth the trouble—spandex leopard-skin pants and a matching top that allowed a healthy portion of her bosom to see the light of day ... or at least the top of her bustier. Despite the allure of her outfit, it was her face that held my attention. She was striking and her brown eyes bore right through me.

"Back for more?"

"As I recall, that was what we were going to discuss."

"So talk."

"Can we go into your office?"

She turned and strode down the hall. I couldn't help but focus on her body. Shapely is the word that comes to mind. I tried to shut my brain off and be in the moment.

She sat down in the chair and pointed to the couch. "What have you got?"

"I may have misled you. I'm not here to talk about you and me per se. I wouldn't mind having that conversation, but right now I'm more interested in discussing the killings. That okay?"

"I knew you weren't here for what you call the 'you-and-me' stuff. Well actually I do, but with you eggheads it takes a while for things to warm up."

"I've never considered myself an egghead. I'm not smart enough."

"You're dumb enough."

"Apparently, but can I ask you a serious question?"

"We weren't being serious? I wouldn't bring you back here if I wasn't sure what you were here for."

"Want to tell me what I'm doing here?"

"You want me to make it easy for you."

"Would you? It would be nice to have something break that way."

"Honey, I could make it so easy for you. And, so hard," she said with a suggestive look.

"Of course you could. So make it easy now, and we'll see about making it hard later."

"Yes, we'll see. For now, I'll tell you some of what you want.

Then you're going to have to leave because it's almost lunchtime, it's Friday, and it's payday. The joint will be jumping soon."

"Very well, what have you got for me?"

"You came here because of the shareholders. Either you figured this out already or this is a gimme, but I'm one of them."

"Thanks. That's news to me. I don't take you for a sucker so whatever you have a share of is worth having a share of. And some of those shareholders are no longer holding their shares so yours is getting larger. So will you tell me anything about the others? Why are they dropping by here? Is there going to be a shareholders' meeting any time soon? How many are there? Will you be there?"

"Slow down, boy. I'm not going to answer all of those."

"Come on, help me out so I can help you out. That's fair. If you're not the killer but you're a shareholder, you might be slated to be joining the dearly departed."

"You believe in fairness? I pegged you for one of those existentialists who pronounce nothing's fair."

"Wait, did you say you pegged me for an existentialist? Am I going to end up really liking you?"

"Didn't I just say slow down?"

"Sorry."

"Here's what I'm going to tell you. Then you're going to be a good boy and leave. And if you come back again, reconsider your priorities."

"I can do that."

"There's going to be a meeting Saturday morning. Those in attendance will share in the investment."

With that she got up and showed me the door.

"Before I go, I have a favor to ask. Can you come to the convention center tonight? I'm going to try and reveal whodunit and it would help to have backup."

"You want me to be backup?"

"Poor choice of words. You're more front and center. But if I need help I'd like to able to reach out to you."

"We'll see. Now goodbye."

"What, no kiss?"

"You got to earn that."

CHAPTER FORTY-FOUR

CHECKING IN

I GOTTA TELL you, my mind was spinning.

FIRST OFF, LET'S be honest, I was very attracted to Nina, despite what my egghead East Coast partially prep-school-educated self was telling me about the likelihood of having a relationship with a brothel owner and possible sex worker. My mother would have a hard time with that. My dad? He'd be worried but he'd be watching. Smart and sexy has always been a turn-on for me, and Nina had both in spades. And even if she wasn't relationship material, I still had a night in town.

There was also the draw of quality time with Louise and Cat. Louise was more fantasy material. As for Cat, I wasn't so sure she was sufficiently interested in me.

I enjoyed Nina's overt flirting. She was definitely interested in me. Though that's probably what every other guy who met her thought; I may be just another John with dough.

That brought the deputy to mind—which put an end to my fantasizing.

There was a board meeting tomorrow morning for shareholders. Given the incentive to reduce the numbers, tonight could be busy.

I wasn't a shareholder, so I wasn't at risk, was I? Unless Boots had invested on my behalf. If I made out well, I'd have to thank him. If I didn't, complaining wouldn't be an option.

Assuming this had to do with shares in his mine, Boots must be aware of all the shareholders even though he indicated he wasn't. Did everyone know everyone? If they did and I was one, I'd be wise to lock myself in my room and come out on Saturday afternoon. Then I remembered that Hopalong, Lone, and Annie had been killed in their rooms.

If Boots wasn't knocking off investors, someone possibly blackmailed the list out of him. Or they were stumbling along, discovering who was involved, and bumping them off along the way. I've experience with that approach.

It would help to have the list. Of course, I could ask people if they were on it. But where would that get me? Even if someone told the truth, I'd have to follow them and wait to see if someone tried to kill them.

The victims had been shot. I could break into everyone's room and try to find a gun, but who'd leave the murder weapon in such an obvious place? It was one thing to break into one room, but when you start doing multiples, your luck can run out quickly. Besides, don't most cowboys have guns?

I headed back to the convention center to make rounds and see what I could pry loose using my own weapon of choice: words.

I hadn't pegged Roy for a smoker but he was standing outside, fidgeting and needing a smoke break. Back in the day, I'd smoked cigarettes. I missed being able to take a time-out and do nothing for five minutes. Then I learned this phrase, "Excuse me, I'm going to take a short break."

Parents tell their kids to take a time-out if they're out of balance. As an adult, you have to call them for yourself.

Roy looked like he wanted to collect himself, but there was still collection work to be done.

I often do my best work when people are off-balance, usually because they're upset, drunk, stoned, or otherwise oft-kilter. You only have to tip the scale and things slip out.

"Hi, Roy. You seem agitated."

"People close to us are getting killed. I could be next."

"Yeah, that's not good. What's behind all this? Why would you be next?"

When I get excited, I'm prone to rush things more than usual. I've been trained not to ask more than one question at a time. You ask one, they answer. You ask two, they can choose which one to answer.

"I'll tell you what I want to be going on—I want to get out of here."

"I imagine you're not alone. Why don't you leave? Do you feel an obligation to stay?"

"Dale won't let us go. She reminded me we gave our word we'd be here and it's here we're going to stay."

"She stands up for her convictions. But that doesn't mean you can't go."

He stared me as if I'd said I was from Mars.

"Obviously you've never been married."

"Point taken. So who's doing this and why would they have it out for you and the others?"

Two questions but at least they were related.

"Beats me. That's what's making me nervous. You ever committed a sin?"

"I haven't killed anyone, but I've crossed the line. How about you?"

"That's just it. I'm not a sinning man. But if someone wants to kill me or any of the others, there's sure to be sin involved."

"What kind of sin?"

"If I'd sinned I'd know what kind. I'd accept why someone had it in for me, but I can't come up with anything."

"Maybe you're not in their sights."

"Or maybe I am, but for a sin I don't know I committed."

"While some people view sin in black and white—good and evil, right and wrong—we therapists are taught to heed gray. What I mean is, what you hold as a sin, or don't hold as a sin, may be seen differently by someone else."

"That's why I'm agitated. Someone could kill me for a sin I don't even know I committed, and they'd never tell me."

"That's unsettling. Would you want someone to tell you why they wanted to kill you? You might think, *Oh, I forgot that. Yeah, that wasn't good.* Or you might think, *What? You're going to kill me for that?*"

"Yes, the whole thing's very disturbing. It's possible I wouldn't want to know. But most likely I would. Either way, I wouldn't die in peace."

"Yeah. That's tough. Years ago, my car flew off the freeway and turned over and over. While I was spinning out of control I said, *This is a stupid way to die.* Fortunately, I was okay, but I drive a lot more carefully now."

"At least you know what you did. You'd have still died mad at yourself. I don't want that."

Yeah, I thought, *but that's what you might get.*

CHAPTER FORTY-FIVE

RANCH GIRL POETRY

THE LOBBY WAS mostly clear, and a new schedule had been posted. Cat had been moved up from the afternoon, and I was relieved I'd returned in time to see her.

There were thirty people in the room. The seat next to Dale was empty. She waved me over and gestured for me to sit next to her.

"Glad Cat hasn't begun yet," I said, sitting down.

"Soon. The meeting threw everything off."

"There was a meeting?"

"Haven't you heard about Annie?"

"Yes, I have. I feel so bad."

"So do we all. They had an impromptu meeting and people spoke."

"I'm sorry I missed that."

"It was sad. Boots was the only one who had stories to tell about her. Everyone else met her this week."

"That is sad."

We sat quietly for a moment, but I had a job to do.

"I have a question. Would it be all right to ask?"

I've said it before, I'll say it again. I ask a question, pause a nanosecond, and continue. It's the illusion of sensitivity I'm show-ing, not the actual stuff.

"Why was she killed?"

"I have no idea."

"Are you worried the killer has you in their sights?"

She gave me a long look. Not quite as incredulous as Roy's when I'd suggested he could leave without her, but close. That's how denial works. If you're in it, you're in it. If she didn't fear she was at risk, she wasn't. Was she similar to Roy and couldn't come up with any sins she'd committed that would warrant that kind of payback? Or did she handle her worry differently? Perhaps she had nothing to worry about. If she and Roy were out for the bigger share, he'd be worried he'd get caught and she'd be planning ahead for a prosper-ous new year.

Cat strode on stage with the kind of assurance I'd like to project but don't. She was grasping the neck of her guitar as she sat down on the stool in front of the microphone.

"Can everyone hear me?"

We could.

"Thank you all for coming. It's been a hard morning, a hard week. None of this was what we were expecting at the first Cowboy Poetry Gathering. Hopefully it won't be the last and the rest will be happier events. Like many of you, I live on a ranch. Life. Death. They're part of our lives. We face hardship all the time. We learn to value life, and that's why we've come together this week."

She got applause for that.

"I have songs, poems, stories I'm going to tell, but first I want to say I've been inspired and touched by the meaningful things I've heard this week, and it's a privilege to be here. We live by a code. We all express it differently, and if you broke it down, parts of the fabric wouldn't stand up to close scrutiny. But we don't overly scrutinize things. We take life as it is and deal with it as it comes. We're all good hands and loyal to the way of life we lead."

She lifted her guitar and played a simple tune with a simple refrain. *We make a stand for the land we love.*

She sang it over and over. It was gentle and forceful. Was she making a stand? Did she mean the cowboy way of life or was she standing up for some other justice?

I didn't like suspecting her of foul play, but I suspected everyone. I'd have preferred by now to have been able to take names off the list. Well, apart from Hopalong, Lone, Duke, and Annie.

My mind wanders. You may have noticed. I reminded myself that I'd had romantic inclinations toward Cat. I ought to pay attention. She told funny, self-deprecating stories and sang songs that described everyday life. Turns out everyday life is how we make our stand. It's the talk we walk.

The audience was appreciative. And so was I, yet my attraction to her was fading. It wasn't her sentiments—I support people standing up for what they believe—but more the realization that she and I led lives that didn't intersect. Of course, the same thing could be said of Nina, but—and I don't like acknowledging this—Nina was a potential adventure rather than a life partner. I'd been regarding Cat in a build-a-life-together way, and that was not in the cards. She wasn't going to leave Missoula, and for the time being I wasn't ready to give up city life for a ranch.

As soon as Cat finished, Dale and a bunch of others approached her. I wanted to approach her as well, but this wasn't the time for anything but compliments.

I waited till the group had thinned down to Dale and a couple of other people I hadn't met. I stood on the periphery and listened in as they weighed the pros and cons of using bran mash for horse colic. Cat said it was all nonsense and did more harm than good, but Dale swore by it. Not caring one way or the other, I tuned out.

I've interrupted other people's conversations to serve my own needs, and I've gotten my fair share of comeuppance for it; so I daydreamed about lunch and whether I'd invite Cat.

"What do you say, Slick?"

"Excuse me, I must have been daydreaming."

"What do you say with respect to making a stand?" Dale asked.

"That was a very powerful refrain. It's one of those things you could interpret in different ways."

"That's what we were debating," said a thin man. "Same as bran mash. There's those that swear by it and others tell you it's hooey."

"Standing up for what you believe is certainly not hooey. It can be dangerous. But so can not standing up for what's important. What were you referring to when you wrote it?"

"We all asked that," said Dale. "But she isn't letting on."

"That's the artist's prerogative. You're not the only artist who wants people to create their own meanings."

Cat smiled.

"Thank you all for the kind words," she said. "I'm glad you enjoyed what I did. I have a lunch date, but I'll see you all later."

With that she hugged the others, then gave me a knowing nod, which told me something and nothing. Then she was gone.

Dale smiled at me. "Want to have lunch together?"

I didn't, but I did.

CHAPTER FORTY-SIX

LUNCH WITH DALE

DALE AND I found a nearby restaurant. She was an attractive woman and even though she was twenty-some years older than me, she still drew a couple of admiring looks which brought a smile to her face. No doubt when she was younger those looks came more frequently.

We ordered our food and got past the superficial. Then I said, "You're a little older than me so I'm hoping you can give me some coaching."

"What's that?"

"When I got into my twenties, the girls I'd admired in high school no longer captured my attention, nor I theirs. Now I'm in my thirties, I still get attention from women in their late twenties, but to the younger ones I'm invisible. I saw a few guys checking you out because you're still a very pretty woman. But you probably don't get the attention you used to. Any tips you want to share about how to deal with this aspect of aging?"

I regretted having said it as soon as it was out of my mouth. I could see the dismay on her face. I'd touched a raw nerve without permission. Just because someone's a trained therapist doesn't mean they've evolved enough to not offend people.

"I don't like your manner."

"I'm sorry. I didn't mean to hurt your feelings."

"No one does. You're correct. I used to get my share of whistles, but they don't come as often as they used to. When you get old, you don't get much of anything."

"That's discouraging to hear. I'm sure it's discouraging to feel."

"It happens bit by bit so you don't take it in at first. Look around you. The majority of people who go out are younger than you. The older you get, the more you don't care about going out, and the more people don't miss you."

"It makes sense on an evolutionary level. It's nature's way of easing the passage."

"It may be nature's way, but it ain't mine. I don't intend to take it lying down."

"I'm all for keeping the spirit alive. Let me change the subject. I've asked you before why are people are being murdered. I can't see a link. Any new insights? What sin did they commit?"

"The sin of living too long."

CHAPTER FORTY-SEVEN

WHAT NOW?

I VALUE THE motivation deadlines provide, though they come with pressure. Still, they do encourage you keep your nose to the grindstone. I wasn't lacking in motivation; I just couldn't find the grindstone.

Dale had kept an eye on the clock so we finished lunch in time to watch Gene do his thing. I still wanted to touch base with him, Buffalo, Boots, and Cat. The sheriff and deputy, too, though I wasn't so eager to speak with them. The lobby was the central point of the convention center. If I holed up there, eventually everyone would pass by and I'd be able to move things forward.

Buffalo came in and I cut him off.

"Hey, have you got a moment?"

"I'm on my way in to see Gene. You should be too."

"I am. I want to quickly touch base first."

"What's on your mind?"

"I'm having trouble figuring out why people were killed. Want to speculate?"

"No I don't."

"Come on, take a guess."

"Obviously, if I had a solid suspicion, I'd tell the police. But I don't. And I don't want to cast aspersions on someone."

"I get that. I don't want to have anyone's reputation sullied, but sharing your hunch may help. These murders are related. They're not crimes of passion per se—there're too many victims in the mix. Is this about greed? Does someone want what others have? If I share my hunch, will you cast an aspersion or two?"

"Let's hear it."

"It has to do with the shares."

"What do you know about them?"

"I know people have them."

"You know who?"

"I know some. Not all. Do you know?"

"I know people have them, but I don't know who or how many."

"What do you know?"

"I know why I got my share and I know what I'm going to do with it."

"Want to tell me?"

"Let's leave it at I'm helping out. That's why I got a share."

"That's kind of you. Want to tell me what the share's in and what you're going to do with it?"

Damn it. That was two questions.

"Let's hold off on that."

"What about casting aspersions? Can you do that?"

"I already did."

"You did?"

He didn't answer as he left to listen to Gene.

When I want to buy a share of an enterprise, I'm hoping it'll lead to profit for me, not as a way of helping out a company. I get that buying stock helps a company but unless someone's investing a substantial amount it won't be that helpful. The way Buffalo had spoken, there may be a different kind of investment involved.

Clarity appeals to me. I get moments of it during the day—when

I'm hungry, thirsty, sleepy. Buffalo's comment left me opaque. I may have been holding those shares in the wrong way. I needed a new angle, a focus. Knowing me, I'd spin out on that and come up with a rainbow of grays.

I WENT TO watch Gene.

Boots, Buffalo, and Gene were on stage, singing a cappella. When they got to *yippie yi yay*, I recognized "Riders in the Sky." If Annie had been there, she'd have thrown in yodeling.

They were given a standing ovation from the adoring forty-strong audience and milked the moment for all it was worth. Gene told the story of how they'd chosen to give the song a try after discovering they'd all seen the film *Riders in the Sky*. Then he heartily thanked them as they left the stage.

Gene settled back into telling stories and reciting poems. It wasn't that they didn't resonate; it was more that, as with Annie, he'd peaked too soon. You get an audience that excited and don't sustain it, the rest of the show pales in comparison. Still he got a standing ovation.

Listening to Gene hadn't pushed me forward with the mystery either. I've come to realize with these mysteries that, unlike in the movies, the clues don't arrive with dramatic background music to alert you.

Roy was sitting in the audience without Dale, waiting for people to clear his row before exiting. Waiting isn't one of my core skills, and the row behind him was empty, so I scooched down it and came up behind him.

"Hey, Roy. Quite a show."

He turned in his seat. "Hello, Slick. How are you?"

"I'm fine, thanks. I got a kick out of seeing Boots and Buffalo up there singing with Gene."

"They have gumption. I wouldn't have gone up there and butchered a classic that way."

"Some in the audience were singing along."

"There's no accounting for taste."

"That's very true. How are you doing? You were agitated before, concerned that the killer might target you for a sin you didn't know you committed. You feeling any better now?"

"Why would I? Did they capture the killer?"

"I haven't heard anything. Until they're caught we're all on edge."

"That's what I told the sheriff. Hurry up and do your job."

"Did you point the finger at anyone?"

"No I didn't, "he said shaking his head. "Did you?"

"Same as you. But I have a suspicion."

"Which is?"

"I'll tell you, but come on, tell me first. You may not want to share your theory with the police until it's more than a theory, but you can tell me. If we merge hunches, we may be able to create a stronger one."

He studied me as if he wasn't sure what to make of me. I can understand that; there are plenty of times I'm not sure what to make of me either. But not this time. I was fishing.

"It has to do with sin," he said.

"You mentioned that before. So did Dale. When you get down to it, most no-nos have to do with sin. Which particular sin is at play here?"

"Envy."

"Want to say more?"

"Someone wants what others have. Is that not envy?"

"It could also be greed."

"All sins are related. Pride, lust, gluttony, wrath, sloth, greed, envy—they're a package deal."

"That's very observant of you, Roy."

"Yes, their sloth could have prompted their wrath. One thing leads to the other. Sin is a pathway with countless stops along the way."

Roy and I were waxing philosophical when Dale showed up. She

CHAPTER THIRTEEN

HISTORY

I RETURNED TO the convention center with a more favorable outlook on life. Boots was conversing with a guy I didn't know. I stood so I'd overhear but appear as if I were respecting their privacy. The guy said he'd read a recent poll of Texas teenagers and they'd rated cowboy at the bottom of a list of desirable jobs. He'd been worried about the turnout so he'd put out sixty chairs so the first poets wouldn't feel bad about all the empty seats. Turned out a few hundred people had showed up, giving him something new to worry about. The free admission helped.

"Slick," Boots said, "as long as you're eavesdropping, let me introduce you to Hal Cannon. He's the director of the Western Folklife Center and one of the main people involved in putting this together."

"Hi, it's a pleasure to meet you. Sorry, I thought I was being inconspicuous. So you expected attendance to be on the low side."

"Good to meet you too. Less than three percent of Americans earn their living through agriculture. When Jefferson was president, it was ninety percent. We're not extinct but we're an endangered species."

"The turnout must be gratifying," I said, pointing to the crowd.

"It is. But numerous people have been working for about five years to make this happen and now we're scrambling to accommodate everyone."

"That's not a bad problem to have. Well done to all."

"Thank you. Movies, singers, and authors have told our story. It was time for this part of American folk literature to have its voice heard … let us speak for ourselves."

"And clearly people want to listen."

"Yes," Hal said with a combination of satisfaction and worry. "When cultures are threatened, people go to the touchstones."

"I didn't know that. Makes sense. When Texas teenagers no longer want to be cowboys, there's a reason to be concerned. I also have a concern. I don't know his actual name, but one of our acting cast, Hopalong, was killed. Do you know why?"

"You'd have to ask Boots."

"Boots?"

"Unless I killed the man, and I didn't, I wouldn't know. I have suspicions, but that's all."

"Willing to share those?"

"Certainly," said Boots as he lowered his voice. "But if I share mine, you share yours. That's fair."

"Let's do that. But I asked first."

"Money is the root of all evil," Boots said with the kind of authority born of experience.

"What kind of money? Gold?"

"Is that your suspicion?"

"Hal knows more but, from what I've been told, there's a bit of a gold rush in Elko. Did Hopalong do some claim-jumping."

"Could be. What do you say, Hal?"

"I didn't know him so it's hard for me to say. I can tell you, it's been quite a while since we had a man for breakfast."

"Being a granola guy," I said, "I'm not familiar with that expression."

"It's a cowboy term," said Boots. "Used to be it was a common occurrence. Even in LA. Someone got shot in a bar at night, and the next morning people would be talking about how such and such place had a couple of men for breakfast."

CHAPTER FOURTEEN

DINNER REHEARSAL

"Good evening, everyone," Boots said as we sat around the dinner table. "I hope you all had an enjoyable day. Planning ahead for Friday night, let's share today's highlights. I'll write 'em down. You don't have to memorize anything but the start time. All you gotta do is spin the highlights I assign you and ad lib when called upon to do so. It'll be fun."

"If you say so," said Annie.

I surveyed the group. She wasn't alone in her uncertainty.

"I do. You'll see. We'll have a fun time. And at least we're all getting free dinners courtesy of the Gathering."

"There's something we can believe in," said Duke.

"Nothing wrong with a free meal. But, come on now, what stood out for you?"

"Georgie Sicking's 'To Be a Top Hand' was inspiring," Buffalo said.

"How so?" Boots asked.

"She talked about how, growing up, she'd wanted to be a top hand but was afraid because she made mistakes. Later, a top hand told her that a 'sorry' hand gets in the way all the time, and a 'good' one once in a while. She didn't worry after that, figuring she was doing fine."

"Just as long as she only got in the way every so often," Annie said.

"I've got a story for you," said Gene. "I was chewing the fat with two guys. It turns out one of them heard about the Gathering the other day. He threw his bedroll in the back of his old Ford and drove here from Montana—he was going to sleep in his car. It didn't occur to him it would be colder here. He froze his butt off last night but this morning he met a guy who offered to share his room. That right there is the cowboy way."

There was a lot of agreement about that. I hadn't known there was a cowboy way. A year ago, I'd found out there was a Dodger way, and there appeared to be overlap when it came to teamwork.

Boots was scribbling away in his notebook when a man hurriedly came up to us and whispered in Boots's ear. Boots excused himself and we set to chatting among ourselves.

I was sitting next to Roy and Duke, who smelled like he'd been smoking his profits.

"Roy, what do you do to amuse yourself?" I asked.

"I write poetry, noodle on the guitar, and try to stay above ground."

"What do you play?"

"On the guitar or are you asking about my favorite board game?"

"You play board games?" Duke asked.

"I'm waiting for that interest to be revitalized when my nephew gets older. These days my playing's mostly with blocks on the floor."

"What do you do to amuse yourself, Slick?" Duke asked.

"A while ago I went to a rodeo in Santa Barbara. That was kinda fun. I also went to Dodgertown in Vero Beach. I haven't gotten back to board games yet."

Boots hurried back into the room. "I'm sorry. I need Slick to come with me. Everyone order dinner and we'll be back soon.

Buffalo, whatever you order for yourself, get for me and Slick too. Let's go."

I'm not that picky an eater so whatever he chose would be fine, although given his bulk, I wouldn't be eating any of the healthier items on the menu. Not that there were many.

We got out into the lobby and Boots said, "It's coming to pass."

"It is?"

"This is what I was worried about. It's the Lone Ranger."

"What about him?"

"He's dead. In his room. Shot, like Hoppy."

"That's horrible."

"You see? This is why I wanted you here. I watched how you did your thing in Vegas. You're the sort people don't take seriously. You can sneak up on them. That's what I need you to do here."

"Okay, I'll take that as a partial compliment. But what gives? Did you tell the police you thought trouble might happen?"

"I couldn't tell the sheriff beforehand. He'd have laughed at me, said we ain't had no bodies for breakfast here in a long time."

"I get that, but still."

"I'd rather you didn't tell anyone this," he said, lowering his voice, "but last week, Maverick was killed."

"Maverick, the TV guy?"

"Yes. No. Months ago I invited a friend to be Maverick. I called him up last week. His wife answered and told me he'd been shot. That's when I got suspicious and that's why I called you."

"Did one of the cast kill Maverick, Hoppy, and Lone?"

"There are a couple of other possibilities but you haven't met them yet," he said as he looked around the lobby to see if any were in attendance. "But, odds are, it's one of our own. That's why it's helpful they're all here together."

"That's a strange approach. If you were worried bringing these people together would lead to someone being killed why not keep them apart from each other?"

"The horse was already out of the barn. Everyone was set to come so I called you."

"Do they know they're all potential suspects?"

"Suspects and victims. They don't have any reason to think that now. But soon, everyone's going to be putting two and two together."

"But surely when that dawns on them, they'll take off. I would."

"That's not the cowboy way. People will want to band together, figure this out, and put a stop to it."

"I don't know about the cowboy way, but I do know a thing or two about human behavior. When the going gets rough, it's flight or fight. Some will stay but most will take off."

"You're the shrink. Do your thing so they don't. We need us all here to resolve this."

"I'll see what I can do. Are you going to go tell everyone now?"

"You can do that. Start earning your keep."

So much for my being invited to attend because of my "attraction" status.

We went back into the dining room and up to the table. One by one, everyone gave Boots their attention, but it was my turn to speak.

"We've got bad news. The Lone Ranger's dead. Not the one on TV. Our Lone Ranger. Like Hopalong, Lone was found shot in his room."

There were gasps. Duke still looked stoned, Gene surprised, Roy confused, Dale shocked, Cat disturbed, Annie upset, and Buffalo angry.

"This is extremely disturbing. We've now lost two of our cast to violent deaths. There's a big part of me that wants to get far away as fast as I can. I wouldn't blame you if you also felt that way. But—and no one knows this better than you—that's not the cowboy way. If someone's taking aim at us, we need to band together to catch that person and put an end to it. If we leave, we won't be able to protect each other. We're more vulnerable apart than we are together."

I didn't get any *hear hears* with that so I pressed on.

"You're all poets. Yes, you have other jobs, but it's the thing that links you. It's your hidden strength. Being a poet is not an easy thing. You have an edge that others don't. You're sensitive and you're calloused. That blend is what's going to forge us together so we can uncover the killer."

While I didn't sense I'd convinced them—heck, I wasn't even positive I'd convinced myself—nobody had left yet, but there was still food to eat.

"Let's take a moment of silence to honor our departed. And when we're done with that, let's track down who did this."

Everyone bowed their head. Well, everyone but me. And Duke. He was peering into the unseen distance.

When the majority were done with their honoring, I said, "Boots has asked us to come together each day to recount our highlights and build the script for the show. These deaths take priority. Let's take time at these sessions to discuss our suspicions. Let's take our fear and turn it into action. What's the connection between Hopalong and Lone? Let's brainstorm."

"I was jawing with Lone about Hopalong this morning," Dale said. "Nothing he said indicated they knew each other."

"Does that ring true for anyone else?" I asked.

Nods.

"Let's assume they didn't know each other before they came here. Anyone have a clue what links them?"

"You said it. We're all poets," Annie said. "I didn't get to meet Hopalong so I don't know anything about him, but Lone was very excited to be here. Well, we're all excited to be here, but he was more so."

"Anyone else get that sense from him?"

Nothing.

I'd had a problem in Dodgertown that was reappearing. Back in LA people come to me for therapy, and I teach grad students how to be therapists. Those people tend to be self-disclosers. They want to talk about themselves. Cowboys and baseball players not so much.

"We're all going to mourn these deaths in our own way. Boots may create a way for us to pay tribute on Friday night. If you have any helpful suggestions please tell me. Boots has made me the unofficial information-gatherer and I want to assist us in getting to the bottom of this."

"You want to do that so you can write a book," said Cat.

Had she been joking with me or busting me? I wasn't sure.

I've learned the Aikido method of therapy—don't push back against incoming forces. Go with the punch.

"There is that. I didn't come here with the intention of writing a book, but, yes, I've written books about going places and people being murdered."

"How do we know you're not the murderer?" asked Buffalo.

More Aikido. "You don't. I can tell you I'm not, but until we unearth who did this, we need to keep an eye on each other."

Boots didn't like that. It didn't fit the bonding ethos.

"Come on. You're all observers of life. That's what poets do. You observe the world, internal and external. It's those skills that'll serve us. Keep an eye out and see what registers. We can do this."

He liked that more.

Me? I still wasn't sure who'd be here for breakfast.

CHAPTER FIFTEEN

HOEDOWN

I'D NEVER BEEN to a hoedown. It's not a big-city thing. Well, that's not true. I've only lived in two—New York and Los Angeles. Both are diverse so there may very well be hoedowns going down, but I hadn't partaken.

Plenty of people had, though. Flared skirts and fancy shirts abounded. I'm not a by-the-book etiquette guy, but I'd noticed how most of the men took off their hats indoors. It appeared the rule, such as it was, didn't extend to dancing. They were either peacocking or didn't know where to safely put their headgear.

When it comes to barn dancing, square dancing, or any kind of dancing with set steps, I'm better off watching. I found my forte in the sixties, when it became acceptable to do your own thing. Beyond that, my skill set peaked with the box step. Fortunately, I was told, anybody could do this, as long as they followed what the caller was saying.

It sounded easy enough, if you're decent at following directions, which I'm not. That said, we were all in a large circle. So far, so good.

I was standing between Roy and Dale and wondering why I wasn't next to Cat.

"Roy, you know your way around the dance floor?"

"Dale and I have been dancing together for years. We go down to the rec center most every week."

"That explains the matching outfits."

"Dale sewed them up herself."

I smiled at her. "Dale, you have some skills."

"Learned from my momma, who learned from hers."

"That's how it often goes. I have to admit, I don't know what I'm doing out here."

"It's too bad you didn't get here early," Dale said. "They had instructions for beginners. But don't worry. They'll get cracking with the mainstream and you'll be fine."

"What takes place after the mainstream?"

"That," said Roy, "is when you'll want to take a rest and let us old hands show you how it's done."

"My pleasure. Have you two been together long?"

"High-school sweethearts," she said.

"Congratulations. Did you meet in poetry class?"

"That'll be the day," Roy said. "Actually, we were introduced by Boots."

"Wow. Did you all go to high school together?"

The music started. Excuse me for glossing over the dancing part. I held my own for the first fifteen minutes, then got winded and confused. I was doing all right with the bowing to your partner, allemandering to the left, and do-si-doing. I even managed to promenade and sashay. But when the caller said to box the gnat, I was ready to watch.

I like to watch. I'm not overly particular though I do have preferences. It goes back to a sign I read as a kid and that's stuck with me: *Work fascinates me. I can sit and look at it for hours.* The people I was watching weren't working, and their joy was palpable.

After a fast song that had everybody hustling to and fro, Cat came over and flopped down. "I'm Marshall Tuckered out."

"Good one. 'Fire on the Mountain' can do that to you."

"Tell me about it."

"I was talking with Roy and Dale. They do this every week. She makes their matching outfits."

"And she does a fine job of it."

"Too bad we're wearing our usual outfits."

She didn't seem to appreciate the remark and said, "It's been a while since I've been to a barn dance."

"Last time I square danced was at summer camp. I had more energy then, and they kept things a bit simpler, though I wasn't any more accomplished."

"Never been to summer camp. Must be nice."

"When you live in the countryside you don't need to go to camp."

"Not when you got chores to do every day."

"Yeah. There is that. Living in the city, the chores we had didn't hold the same necessity. My parents wanted to get us out of the house and let us know there were forests, mountains, and lakes in the world."

"I can see why they'd want you out of the house for a while," she said, making sure not to look at me.

"Ouch. I want to believe it was more about nature than not wanting me at home, but I know I take some getting used to."

"If you say so."

"Are you giving me a hard time because you like me, or is it something else?"

"Both."

"Want to say more?"

She looked at me for a moment before saying, "Not really"

"I'll go with the half-full part of that."

"You do that."

"I have a question for you."

"Shoot."

"Truthfully, I have more than one. I haven't sorted through them and put them in order."

"Go on."

"I realize we hardly know each other, and relationships evolve as you share experiences and discover more about each other, but on the face of it, what are my prospects with you?"

"Whoa. I didn't see that coming," she said, giving me the briefest smile. "Well, I did. But not quite so soon."

"If we do spend more time together, you'll find out that foreplay is one more thing I don't do well."

"Try upgrading those skills."

"That's been mentioned before. I've even said it to myself, but I have different forces at play that make it challenging for me."

"Not just you. Your approach, while it has a certain charm, lacks substance."

"Yeah. I get that too. Listening to me, I'm not sure I'd want to date me."

"I'll tell you what. When I go back out on the dance floor, see if you can upgrade your social skills. I'm intrigued, but need to know more before I'm prepared to shift those gears."

It wasn't a win. But it wasn't a loss. At the end of the night would I be listening to "Heard It in a Love Song"? Or would I be like "This Ol' Cowboy," who'd once again spent the night alone?

CHAPTER SIXTEEN

MOONSHINE

I UNDERSTAND THE value of letting things evolve organically. I can even walk that walk now and then, but usually not with women. I want to know right away if I have a good chance so I can relax a little. When I try to be on my best behavior for extended periods, I don't enjoy myself. Others might enjoy me more, but it's not a win–win. And, yes, if I slowed down, they'd be more inclined to consider me, but they may as well get a taste of what they're in for sooner rather than later.

I was mulling over my next steps with Cat when Annie sat down beside her.

"I'm bushed," she said. "I need a break. How you two doing?"

I took some comfort in her referring to us as *you two*. Hopefully what she saw I'd get to see. Before I could, Buffalo and Duke came over. I hadn't seen them on the dance floor. They smelled like they'd been on the bar floor.

"Howdy, everyone," Duke said in a voice more jovial than usual. "How's everyone doing?"

"You boys been holding down the fort over at one of the local watering holes?" Cat asked.

"Didn't need to," said Buffalo. He pulled a flask out of his hip pocket, then slipped it back in. "Me and Duke been sitting out in my truck gazing at the stars and getting acquainted."

"Learn anything of interest?" I asked, curious if Buffalo had also been getting acquainted with the Prairie Gold.

"Buffalo knows how to make his own moonshine."

"From all appearances, you know what you're doing," I said.

"Been brewing it forever. Learned it from my pappy, he learned it from his."

"Admirable to pass along family traditions," I said.

I got some looks, but that's the thing about being a part-time wiseass—people are not always sure whether to be offended or not.

"I'm going to go kick up my heels," Cat said, and skipped onto the dance floor.

"I'm coming with you," said Duke.

I wanted to flirt more with her, but wouldn't score any points on the dance floor.

I turned to Annie and Buffalo. "You two know each other?"

"Met here for the first time," said Annie. "But now that I know that Buffalo has certain skills, I'm inclined to know him more."

"You two want to go outside and get acquainted?" Buffalo tapped his hip pocket.

"I'd be delighted," said Annie.

"Count me in," I said.

I'm not a big drinker and I'd never had moonshine, but like any educator, I'm open to expanding my knowledge base.

We wasted no time getting to the rusty Chevy I'd followed to the gold mine. If it had been warmer, we could have stood outside, but the temperature was approaching single digits and I was content to be in the warmer environs of Buffalo's well-worn pickup. We piled into the front seat, Annie in the middle.

When it comes to cleanliness I'm not too OCD, but having

quickly glimpsed the fast-food bags, candy bars, and assorted detritus, I kicked them aside.

"Here you go," said Buffalo, handing Annie his flask. "Wet your whistle."

She tilted her head back, took a sizable swig, and let out a howl that would have made a coyote proud. Wanting to be one of the gang, I refrained from wiping the spout, figuring the alcohol would kill any germs if it didn't kill me. I took a pull big enough not to look like a teetotaler but small enough not to dissolve my liver.

I don't know what was in that flask, but my moon was blazing. My eyes rolled back, my jaw yawned wider than I'd imagined was physically possible, and my body began to shake. Then I made Annie's coyote sound like a mouse.

"You feeling the love?" Buffalo asked, and took a huge gulp.

"I'm not positive it's love I'm feeling, but I've never felt this way before. What the hell's in this?" I was warm all over.

"It's corn liquor, isn't it?" Annie said.

"It's a secret family recipe. Guaranteed to cure what ails you."

"The next time I feel my body, I know it'll be ailing, but right now, that's some mind–body enhancing firewater," I said. "If I wanted to become a full-blown alcoholic, I'd raid your still."

"We'd shoot you like the rest," Buffalo said.

Alcoholic may not have been the best word to use. But, truthfully, I didn't care. Still, I made a note not to raid the still.

"Not that I want to raid your still," said Annie, "but where do you live?"

"She wants to know because we're used to seeing those Coors ads where it's all about the water. And wherever you're making this stuff, you must have mighty fine water."

I'm a cheap drunk. I was off my game. Whatever sleuthing I may have carried forth was passing over my conscious mind. I could only hope it would land in my subconscious because whatever we said or did after that, I don't remember.

CHAPTER SEVENTEEN

COMEUPPANCE

Tuesday January 29, 1985

I LIKE TO get up early and engage with the day. Most days, my internal alarm clock wakes me up close to six. It did that this morning, but I rolled over and went back to sleep. I got up at nine, feeling better than I had at six, but not anywhere close to passable. I still had my clothes on and hadn't made it under the covers.

I undressed and made it to the bathroom in time to throw up. Then I stumbled into the shower. I know we're supposed to be water-wise, but any conservation consciousness had left the premises; I could barely move.

I don't know the cure for hangovers but it probably includes aspirin, coffee, and a bit of the hair of the dog. I wasn't inclined to do anything, especially the dog part. I slowly eased myself down to the cafeteria, had a piece of toast, coffee, and aspirin, and returned to my room for a nap.

Whatever I'd done the night before, I wasn't going to do it again. Ever. Unless it turned out to be worth the pain.

A cowboy hat lay among the clothes I'd shed on the floor. Evidently I'd been shopping.

When I got back up close to noon, I took another shower, downed more coffee and aspirin, and added a BLT into the mix. That was as fortified as I was going to get. I reluctantly made my way over to the convention center.

I wanted to sit in the back, listen, and doze off. Enter the world gently. No sooner had I gotten into the lobby than Boots was heading my way.

"Where have you been? I've been going crazy."

"I had a bit of a slow start. I had too much of Buffalo's moonshine."

"Any of that's too much. It'll take the paint off your car."

"His car did look like he'd spilled some on it."

"Live and learn. In the meantime, we've got serious trouble."

"Someone else been killed?"

"Worse."

"Worse?"

"That's an exaggeration. Worse for me. Somebody stole my hat. When I catch the son-of-a-bitch, I'm going to skin him alive."

However lousy I'd been feeling before, I'd just doubled-down. Being skinned alive is no doubt worse than a moonshine hangover. I'd definitely want to be fortified by that paint remover first.

"That's terrible? How did it happen?"

"That's the thing. I was hoofing it on the dance floor and took off my hat. No cowboy would ever steal another man's hat. Next thing I know, it's gone. The lowlife rustler who stole my pride and joy is enjoying his last days."

I can't say I was enjoying my last days, but elected not to share that information with Boots.

"I'll keep an eye out."

"You do that."

I'd had the opportunity to tell Boots the truth but had neglected to seize the moment. He'd have forgiven me. Or he'd have whipped out his bowie knife and skinned me on the spot.

One of the problems with lying is you tell one, you have to tell more to cover the first one. That's a whole new narrative you need to remember. It's simpler if not easier to tell the truth. I can talk that talk but don't manage to consistently walk it.

I needed to cover my ass and spin as few lies as possible. I had a new priority: get Boots's hat back to him. I could drop it somewhere and have someone else run across it, but what if they kept it? That wouldn't be good. No, I wanted to make sure he got it back, and that meant putting it in his room.

I don't consider myself a thief, but given some of the actions I've taken since I became involved in solving mysteries, I've had to stop holding myself out as a law-abiding citizen. Now, I opt for rule bending. Okay, rule breaking. And after all, I wasn't breaking in to steal anything, just return what I'd already stolen.

The legal and ethical hurdles weren't holding me back. Figuring how to break into his room, and the propitious moment to do it, was. Those who've traveled down this highway with me before know I've acquired skills in this area. Nothing worthy of an entry on my résumé but sufficient to give me options about how to approach the situation.

I made my way to one of the bulletin boards and scanned the schedule. Boots was performing tomorrow morning. If I stayed away from the moonshine tonight, I'd make my move then. How I'd do it would be the challenge. I'd succeeded in Vegas by telling the person at the front desk I'd mislaid my key, but in a small town, that kind of anonymity is hard to come by.

I'd deal with that later. Now, I'd sit down, listen to poetry, and take a nap. One thing I learned in school was how to appear attentive and nap at the same time. I sat and paid marginal attention to Joaquin Quadra as he told a story involving his adventures south of the border with the bandidos and police. I was languishing in that space where you can barely hear voices and can't discern the words.

"Here you go."

I opened my eyes.

A teenage cowgirl handed me a piece of paper. Everyone was holding one.

"Please," said Joaquin. "Join with someone and finish the rest of the poem."

I wanted to finish my nap but Annie sat down next to me.

"You don't look so hot," she said.

"That matches how I feel. I had a bit too much moonshine last night."

"You got that right. I'm surprised you showed your face."

"Do you know what I did?"

"You don't know?"

"If I did, I might be on my way home. But I don't remember anything after taking a swig of that moonshine. Heck, I may have stolen his flask and finished it off."

"Oh, you did worse than that."

"Great. Want to tell me or should I wait for someone to come punch me out?"

"You don't need to worry about that. Cat's not the type."

"Wait. Wait. Wait. What did I do?"

"I don't know."

"But you said you were surprised I'd showed my face."

"I was messing with you. I don't know what you did, but I do know you've got repair work to do with Cat."

"What did she say?"

"It's not what she said, although she did say you were a jerk. It's more the embarrassment and frustration she had to endure."

"Jerk I can deal with. It's not the first time. What was she embarrassed and frustrated about?"

"You'll have to ask her. What about the fragment?"

"The fragment?"

"In your hand. The poem we were asked to finish."

"Oh. Let me read it. I may not be of any help."

"I see."

I took a moment and read the poem. The two lines threw me off.

Angel in a Cowboy Hat.
We put that on his tombstone.

Given my apparent misdeeds, I doubted Boots or Cat would be inclined to use the word "angel" in relation to me. But mostly I was hoping I wasn't going to end this trip with a tombstone.

CHAPTER EIGHTEEN

COMFORT FOOD

You ever want to treat yourself? Maybe as a reward for an achievement or a way of consoling yourself when things have not gone well. As a kid, I was underweight. I was lucky to go to a summer camp with an after-lunch nap on the schedule. After napping, I'd report to the nurse's office for a malted milkshake. It was a health regime I took a liking to, but as with so many of the things I liked in my youth, I rarely get to follow through and live my adult life as a child. Although I do retain elements.

I'd had two naps so I sat at the counter of the hotel coffee shop, slurping my malt. I'd soothed myself further by ordering a side of fries.

"Hey, jackass, mind if I join you?" asked Cat.

"Please. I need to make amends. Want some fries?"

She took one, dipped it in the catsup I'd squirted on the plate, and sat down next to me.

"I need to confess something," I said.

"You'll need to go to church for that."

"Want more fries?"

She did.

"Want some malt? It's chocolate."

She got a straw, put it in my glass, and took a healthy sip.

"By the way, you look exceptional today."

"That's not helping."

"Here's my story. Annie told me that I did things last night for which I need to make reparations. I'm very invested in apologizing. But here's the truth. Whatever I did, I have no memory of doing. All I remember is drinking moonshine in Buffalo's pickup with him and Annie. Then I woke up in my bed. That's it. Whatever I did, I'm sorry I did. That is, if you want me to be sorry. Want more malt?"

"It's awfully convenient not remembering anything."

"It is and it isn't. I've never blacked out before. That's not my style. I prefer to be in control. I'm very sorry if I stepped out of bounds. Want to tell me what I did? It might refresh my memory."

She asked the waitress for a glass and poured the remaining malt from the cup into it, then got to work on the fries.

"You hurt me."

"Really? I physically hurt you? That'd be totally out of character."

"No, you embarrassed me. You made a fool of yourself, and in so doing made a fool of me."

"That sounds more like my speed. I'm not a stranger to making a fool of myself. Want to tell me what I did?"

"It's not what you did. Some said it was cute, but you had no regard for how it affected me. I get that you're attracted to me and want to woo me. You made that perfectly clear last night. It was one thing when you spoke to me privately. It's embarrassing when you do it in front of others."

"I get that and I'm sorry. What I did to try to impress you wasn't well thought out."

"Or acted out. You need to upgrade your skills if you're going to try to be Cyrano."

"Huh? Did I wax unpoetic?"

"More than that. You"—she ate more fries, drank more malt, and made me wait her out—"paraded, well, stumbled back to the hotel, 'escorting' me safely home. When we got to the hotel, you climbed up onto the desk and …"

"Yes?"

"You chanted your ode to the 'splendors' of me. At first it was funny, but it went on and on. The receptionist tried to pull you down but you insisted on standing your ground, or trying to. A crowd gathered and cheered you on, and that emboldened you."

"Not good, huh?"

"Not good poetry. And you can't sing. Thankfully, when you started to dance, you fell off the counter and passed out. That's when I told them your name and left."

I was going to say there were worse things, but this wasn't the time to minimize my actions. Humor's a defense I often use to take the edge off, but I needed to take my comeuppance.

"I'm sorry. I was thoughtless. And I have no singing chops."

Someone I didn't know lumbered by and slapped me on the back. "Nice show last night. Now my wife wants me to proclaim myself the same way."

"Thanks. She may want to think twice about it. I'm not convinced the recipient of my affections was all that pleased."

"Well, she oughta be. You're a lousy poet and singer, but you sure know how to declare yourself. Now I gotta perform for the old lady."

I tried to contain my pleasure.

"Don't be all full of yourself," Cat said. "Just because someone states you were funny doesn't mean it's a fully held opinion."

"I only wanted you to know how badly I was smitten."

"Well, now I and a bunch of strangers all know."

CHAPTER NINETEEN

DINNER REHEARSAL

HEARING ABOUT MY hotel-lobby adventures had made me gun-shy about what else I might discover. The good news was Boots didn't know I was to blame for his missing hat. The bad news was I wasn't making any inroads with Cat.

I was the last person to arrive for our daily review. I took a seat at the end of the table. Roy welcomed me with a good-ole-boy punch to my upper arm. I'd made inroads with someone although wasn't clear what I'd done to deserve it. I gave him a knowing nod but had no clue what I was acknowledging.

"Now that we're all here," Boots said, staring at me sternly, "let's recount the highlights of the day. I'll go first. My highlight, as you all know, was a lowlight by a lowlife last night. I'm going to include it in the show along with the lynching when we grab the scoundrel. I have to admit, I'm in a bad mood and nothing's going to make it better until I have my reckoning."

"You're damn right," Buffalo said. "We all understand. Somebody who isn't living the cowboy way is counting their days."

Ay yai yai. Things were not improving. Had I been wearing the hat when I serenaded Cat? I didn't like that picture but couldn't shake it. Still, if you can't beat 'em, you need to join 'em. I didn't even know what the cowboy way entailed, never mind abided by it, but I needed to show I was on board.

"Not being a hat-wearer, I don't fully appreciate its value, but I do understand that there are rules of conduct in a community. Someone isn't a member in good standing. Possibly the same person who killed our colleagues."

Where I come from, that's called a diversion tactic. It was working until Roy said, "Stealing a man's hat kills his soul."

I'd wanted to change the subject, but focused instead on keeping my anxiety in check. A close friend, who's also a therapist, told me that when his clients are having anxiety attacks, he tells them to ask themselves one question: Am I in danger?

I wasn't in danger now, but if I couldn't get that hat into Boots's room without being detected …

"I've got a highlight," I said. "Or a lowlight, depending on your point of view. Last night, I had my first experience with moonshine."

"And lived to tell the tale," said Buffalo.

Yeah, but for how long?

"Not sure that's going to make the cut," Boots said.

"The kid lost his cherry last night, Boots," Duke said. "We need to give him his due."

"People say you put on quite the show in the lobby," Dale said.

I smiled weakly.

"Not all the reviews were favorable," Annie needed to add.

"Let's not include it in the show," I said. "I bet others have worthier contributions."

As the others chipped in with their own stories, my mind drifted to Cat. I'd embarrassed her, certainly, and she'd made it clear she hadn't valued what I'd done. But part of me felt she kinda liked it too. Wishful thinking? Wouldn't be the first time. She'd eaten the fries and malt and hadn't told me to stay away from her, so there was that, but what else was there?

CHAPTER TWENTY

A SOBER NIGHT

I KNOW WHEN I need to walk the straight and narrow. While a part of me wanted to escape from how I felt and what others felt about me, drugs and alcohol weren't the path. At least not tonight. I wanted to get a good night's sleep so I could make my penance during Boots's performance.

It was Tuesday night. That's a school night. The poetry reading at the convention center wasn't calling me; *The Riders of High Rock* was waiting in my room if I wanted to get away from my worries and read about someone else's.

I'm not that interested in gambling. I'd be more interested if my efforts garnered rewards, but I've neither skill nor luck when it comes to playing cards with friends or pulling the handle on a slot machine. When I do gamble, I locate the machine with the biggest payoff and the worst odds, and give it my money in hopes that I'll get the big payoff that will make a significant difference in my life. After all, my odds are the same as the eventual winner's.

I've still haven't gotten that apartment in Paris, houseboat in Amsterdam, and yacht in the Caribbean, but I got twenty dollars' worth of quarters anyway. The joint wasn't exactly jumping. Most of those in attendance looked like they were living close to the fault line, which didn't do much for my spirits.

I made the acquaintance of a machine with a $20,000 jackpot. It wouldn't rock my world but it would get me a new sports car. In the healing-arts world, hope is an important ally. According to my favorite therapist author, Irvin Yalom, MD, the "instillation of hope" is the number-one curative factor. When you give up hope, you give up. When you have hope, you're optimistic, and that improves your mindset and engages your body more actively in healing. I'm not here to promote his books, but if you enjoy the application of psychology go check out *Love's Executioner* or *Lying on the Couch*.

I sat in front of the slot machine with a small degree of hope; the odds were against me but before I sat down I'd had no immediate hope of coming into $20,000. Now, I had a chance.

It almost took five minutes for my hope to leave the premises. Five minutes after that, Annie came my way.

"Hey, Slick, how you doing?"

"Aside from losing my chance to get a new car, I'm ready to go bed."

"You got after it pretty hard last night."

"Can you fill me in some more? I don't remember anything beyond the pickup."

"Well, we did sit there for a while. Buffalo's got a lot of storyteller in him and a lot of backup shine in the bed."

"I'm guessing I took more than that first hit. What's in that stuff? I may have lost a quadrant of my brain cells."

"You don't want to ask those kinds of questions. And Buffalo ain't gonna answer them."

"All right. Just tell me what I did and who else I owe an apology."

"If I were you I'd tell Buffalo I was joking about moving in with him. That spooked him."

"It spooks me."

"He figured it was the shine talking."

"What else did I say?"

"To tell you the truth, I lost track of you back at the hoedown. You were kickin' up your heels a bit. You weren't following along. This kind of dancing is more prescriptive than you're used to."

"That's for sure. So was I doing my own thing?"

"That's a nice way to put it. They had to relegate you to the sidelines when you set about yodeling."

"This is embarrassing. Were people upset with me?"

"Well, you gotta remember, we're talking about cowboys here. You weren't the only drunk guy in the corner singing, yodeling, and dancing. Heck, you made new friends. Not that any of you'd remember that."

"Anything else you want to tell me before I hide in my room?"

"Tomorrow is another day."

CHAPTER TWENTY-ONE

MORNING ACTIVITIES

Wednesday January 30, 1985

I HAD NO clue why Maverick, Hopalong, or Lone were killed or how to go about learning more. I've experienced the pitfalls of assuming things, but they can be a time-saver. They can also be a time-loser if you're wrong. Being a guy who tries to save time, I'm not unfamiliar with letting assumptions guide me till they leave me short. I was banking on the killings being connected. How and why? Those assumptions had yet to arrive.

There are crimes of passion, but I couldn't see anyone being that passionate about Lone to want to kill him. And Hoppy and Maverick too? The killer would need an abundance of passion. No, I was ruling that out. Following the money trail was a more viable angle, but first I had to find it.

I had one lead. Boots. He'd orchestrated our coming together. He knew way more about what was happening than he'd told me. I needed to have a serious conversation with him. But first I needed to return his hat. My initial plan had been: Get into his room, leave the hat, and get out in the shortest amount of time.

Now I added searching his room. It could give me more

information; it could also get me in more trouble. I'd drive over to the convention center in time for his 10:00 a.m. performance and make sure he saw me. As soon as he got up to speak, I'd haul ass back to the hotel and do my breaking and entering. All I needed to do was to sneak into his room and not to overstay my welcome.

After breakfast, I explored the hallway outside Boots's and my rooms. One door had a *No Entrance* sign on it. I knocked on it. When no one answered I went in. There were the usual shelves with towels, sheets, and toiletries, and a cart with its own supplies and a key hanging off the corner. *Easy*, I said. Then wished I hadn't, worrying I'd jinxed myself.

I got in my car and drove the mile and a half to the convention center. A sober night's sleep had left me feeling as good as I could about the activities ahead.

That didn't last long.

Boots came up to me in the lobby. "I want to be straight with you."

"Please," I said, not pleased.

"I'm disappointed in you. I brought you here to help out and you ain't done diddly."

Our definitions of doing diddly didn't totally match. Some reparative work was in order.

"I'm sorry I've disappointed you. What's the matter, boss?"

"I expect you to brief me about your progress. The other night you made a fool of yourself, and last night you were nowhere to be found. I made a mistake bringing you here."

"Let's not be hasty. Why don't we meet for lunch after your performance? I've got things I want to run by you."

He wasn't mollified, but we arranged to meet at the Giddy Up.

Other people came up to him and he got distracted. I made my way toward the room where he'd do his thing. He'd drawn a sizable audience, and I stood in the hallway with a partial view of the stage. When he took to the stage I took off.

I was back in the second-floor hallway in no time. I sauntered down to the *No Entrance* room and knocked. No answer. I slipped in. And slipped out. The cart was gone. My already-churning adrenaline shifted up a gear. I shed my sauntering and sprinted down the hallway, quickly glancing into any open rooms. No sign of the cart.

I tried to come up with a plan B, upset with myself for not having at least sketched out one previously. Then a woman got out of the elevator with the cart.

"I'm relieved to see you," I said. "I locked myself out of my room and was on my way to the lobby to get a key. Can you help me? I'm in kind of a hurry."

"Certainly," she said. "Which room?"

I couldn't remember the number. "Here, I'll show you."

She let me in.

Boots's room replicated mine. The difference was that his had a typewriter on the table, with stacks of paper—typed and untyped—next to it. I glanced at the sheets. Our scripts. They were mostly empty.

There was a notebook, and I thumbed through it. The pages were filled with graphs, maps, lists, and other notations that made little sense.

I stuck my head out the door. The cart was at the far end without the maid. I slipped off my shoes and put them in the doorway and hauled ass to my room. I grabbed the hat and stepped back out into the hallway. The maid was standing by her cart.

I waved to her and said to my closing door, "Thanks, I'll see you later," then went back to Boots's room. I put the hat on his bed, put on my shoes, took one last look and made my getaway.

The maid was gone and soon I was too. I got back in the car, wiped the sweat off my brow, took several deep breaths, and tried not to be too taken with myself as I sped back to the convention center.

I wanted to slip in to Boots's performance so I'd be able to compliment him about his poetry later. That way, he'd be less apt to put two and two together when he found his hat. The podium faced the door so getting in unseen was not going to happen. I'd have to tell a lie about being called away by a client in crisis.

"Last night I was in the Stockmen's bar and you won't believe who came into the place. It was the past." Boots spoke with feigned astonishment. "He seemed very old and misunderstood. And, worst of all, he was upset how things had turned out. Then, who comes storming in? None other than the present? Folks, let me tell you, the present was even more upset with the past for the way they left things. Trouble was brewing. You could feel it all over the place. Then, who came charging into the place, but the future. He glared at the two of them with anger and resentment for the mess they were going to leave him. Things were about to explode. I tell you, friends, things were very tense in there."

It took a moment, but people laughed. I'd have enjoyed it more if he hadn't been scowling at me when he said it. It made me very tense.

He told more jokes and stories, then invited Gene up to the stage. Gene was dressed up in what I assumed was his costume—pristine white hat, fancy shirt, and guitar.

"Ladies and gentlemen, you may have already met Phil Marcoe. He'll be playing the part of Gene Autry in our show this Friday. We wanted to sing you a song and you're welcome to join in."

It wasn't a surprise what song they chose—"Back in the Saddle Again."

CHAPTER TWENTY-TWO

LUNCH DATE

I WAS WAITING at the Giddy Up for Boots to show up. Waiting's one of those things I don't enjoy but get plenty of opportunities to improve my skills.

Boots showed up a reasonable amount of time after he said he would. If he hadn't been my boss I'd have mentioned it, but given that I was already in the doghouse I kept my persnickety tendencies to myself.

"They've got a tasty chicken-fried steak," he said as he sat down.

"Thanks for the tip. I'm going to stick with the cheeseburger."

"Suit yourself. So, where are we? And how come you came in late to my performance?"

"Sorry I missed some of it. I was looking forward to seeing you and what I saw was great. You're very talented. But ..." I said, taking my beeper off and showing it to him, "ever since I got this thing, clients call me at all hours. It's reassuring for them to be able to get hold of me when they're in crisis, but it does interfere."

"You need to give me that number so I can reach you."

"I can do that," I said, trying to hide my dismay with an eager smile. In truth, I'd gotten the beeper so my mother and father could call me in an emergency.

He ordered chicken-fried steak and I got my cheeseburger with fries and a Diet Coke.

"You told me you had things to run by me."

"I do. I'm having trouble putting the pieces together. Maverick was killed before we got here, Hopalong before our first dinner together, then Lone. What do they have in common aside from being a part of the cast?"

"I was wondering when you'd get around to asking me that."

"Wonder no more. What's the deal?"

"That's hard to answer. I do have a hunch but I can't tell you. I'd like to cuz it would give you a leg up, but I'm duty-bound not to."

"Hold on. You want me to stop the killings, but you're not going to tell me something that could help me out?"

"It ain't that hard. You're the slick one—you'll put it together."

"Thank you for the vote of confidence, but, if I remember correctly, you were upset I wasn't moving along faster."

"This ain't rocket science. You gotta understand cowboys see the world in black and white. You shrinks are all about the gray. Make things easy on yourself. Look at this the way we'd look at it."

"I can try that. Anything else?"

"I can't tell you more."

"Just so I'm clear, is the reason you can't tell me because you killed them and you don't want me to out you even though at some level you do?"

"There you go again. Looking for the gray. This ain't that complicated. I may tell corny jokes and not be the best poet in town, but I'm not that stupid to hire you to catch me."

"I get it. There are things you're aware of but can't tell me. So why can't you tell me?"

"I can't help you with that either."

I was becoming frustrated, and it must have showed on my face.

"I've told you all you need to know. The fact that you don't know more means you're not asking the right people the right questions. I thought you were smart. You're a shrink. You're supposed to be able to get people to open up. Do your job, then someone will tell you what I can't and you can solve this."

"I only need to get people to tell me what you won't tell me. Is it okay if I tell them you won't tell me?"

"I can't believe you'd think that was a good way to go."

"I hear you. But I'm the kind of guy that keeps throwing things at the target to see what lands."

"You crash-landed. You need to live up to your name rather than fumbling about like Clouseau."

CHAPTER TWENTY-THREE

WHY FOLLOW ADVICE?

GOOD ADVICE CAN go in one ear and out the other. It's not that Boots's suggestion wasn't worth heeding. I simply had other things I wanted to do this afternoon.

He went back to the convention center and I used the pay phone in the Giddy Up to call Gus. He agreed to meet me at the hotel at two and gave me directions to a hardware store.

On the way back to the hotel, I stopped and picked up a pickaxe and a pair of gloves.

I needed to change my clothes and get the flashlight out of my gumshoe kit. Outside the home I try to project a more professional, if partially deceptive, image. Unless I'm camping, I don't bring my well-worn clothes. That didn't leave me with optimal options, so I slipped on the T-shirt I'd been wearing when I left LA and the jeans I'd slept in.

When Gus picked me up, I was ready to go exploring.

"Where we off to?"

"I want to go back to that mine."

"No problem. How come you don't drive yourself?"

"Two reasons. When I drive, I pay closer attention to where I'm going. I'm not convinced I can remember where to turn off."

"I remember. And the second reason?"

"I'm hoping there'll be no one there and I can explore inside."

"You want to be careful about being in someone else's mine with a pickaxe. People get shot for that."

"That's both good and not good to know, and directly relates to why I wanted to have you drive me."

"You want me to go in there with you and take a bullet for you?"

"Would you?"

He vigorously shook his head. He might have been weighing turning back.

"Lucky warned me about you. I should have listened."

"I was joking. No, I don't want you to go in there with me. And while I'd appreciate your taking a bullet for me, I'd prefer neither of us got shot."

"So …?"

"So how about you drive me up there? We stop where we did before. I take a peek. If no cars are there, I go into the mine. You park in front of the mine and stay there. If you see someone coming, you honk the horn. I'll ditch the pickaxe, run to the entrance, and be standing there admiring it when whoever shows up."

"Sounds sketchy."

"Most of my plans have that element to them."

"It's a hundred a day like we agreed."

"If I ask you to risk taking that bullet we can—"

"Double everything. And don't forget Betsy."

When was the last time you were in a gold mine? I've seen them in movies, but as with many things in the movies, the real deal was filthier and had more character—if you consider spiderwebs, trash, puddles of unknown substances, and noxious smells to add character.

It didn't take long before I took out my flashlight complete with new batteries.

The mine was bleak and kept on going longer than I'd envisioned. Had Buffalo and whoever had been here with him been assessing whether there was any mojo left in it?

I felt kind of stupid with my pickaxe because I had no idea of where to put it to use aside from at the end. I'd come to one fork so far and had opted for left. The reason? Most people are right-handed. The person who'd dug this would have been more inclined to go right. When that didn't work out, they'd go back a ways and head left. That would put the most recent digging to the left. I was overthinking, but what else is new?

If I didn't run into anymore forks, I'd be able to make my way out as long as the flashlight held up. String tied to the entrance and my wrist would have provided greater reassurance, and more choice. I made a mental note.

I'd assumed I'd recognize new mining when I stumbled upon it. There were places along the wall that appeared to have received recent whacks, but it was hard to distinguish the new from the old. Could just be the wall caving in.

Either I'd gone further or sound doesn't travel that well in a mine. Which is why I didn't hear the car horn.

All I heard was, "Where the hell are you?"

I had a split-second choice—call out as if it were no big deal or keep my mouth shut.

I opted for the bad decision—and kept quiet.

There was a pause, then the voice said, "I know someone's here. Where are you?"

Yikes. Had Gus already taken a bullet for me?

I gently discarded the pickaxe and the gloves, and called out, "Whew. Glad you came. I'm over here."

Some of that was true.

The footsteps were coming closer. I started toward them, then stopped. I ought not get too far away from that pickaxe. A flashlight beam bounced off the walls, and as they came into view, I took a couple of strides forward so they'd see me coming their way.

"So relieved you showed up. I was getting claustrophobic. I didn't realize this mine went on and on."

"What the hell are you doing here?" Duke said.

"That's a very astute question. I'm unclear on that myself. What are you doing here?"

"I'm here for my own reasons. What are yours?"

"My reasons are my own as well. But I'll share if you'll reciprocate."

"Boots said you were an outsider. Are you part of this?"

"No more than you. What part of this are you part of?"

"Don't give me that runaround. Are you a shareholder?"

"I have shares in some things. How about you? You a shareholder?"

"I have shares in some things as well. You want to quit this fancy-footing and tell me what you're doing here?"

"Of course. I'm not much of a dancer. But you already know that."

"Quit stalling."

I wasn't sure how to proceed. Not that that ever stops me. But Duke wasn't holding a gun, unless his flashlight had James Bond gadgetry. Still, Boots had assigned us roles based on our qualities, and while Duke didn't exactly look like John Wayne, he was tall enough and big enough to beat me up and leave me here with the rest of the discarded garbage.

"I was here the other day with someone whose privacy I need to respect. But I left wanting to learn more so decided to come back."

"That's a slippery answer, Slick."

"I'm a therapist and we're all about protecting people's identities. If I told you more, I'd be compromising their confidentiality, and that wouldn't be good for business."

"Were you here with Buffalo?" He asked, pointing his flashlight in my eyes.

"I didn't say that. You're free to make whatever you want of what I said. What are you doing here?"

"I could say the same bullshit crap you said."

"But you're better than that."

"That's true. Let's just say I'm checking out my investment."

"Wait, you own this?"

"I didn't say that, but you're free to make whatever you want of what I said."

"I'm supposed to be the smart aleck here. Do you actually own this?"

"Let's leave it at I'm checking out my investment."

"Very well," I said and shined my light on the walls. "So how's your investment checking out? Is it going to assist you with your retirement, let you get that big spread with your own brand?"

"That's what I was checking until I found a claim-jumper."

"I'm not much of a jumper. I'm more of a stepper. But I can assure you, I'm not here to stake a claim."

"If you were we'd have to put together a lynching party."

"That's a party I'd prefer to skip. You want to continue checking things out? I'm happy to accompany you."

"I bet you are. Why don't you skedaddle out of here before I decide to start the party."

"You bet."

I skedaddled out while I still could.

Gus was asleep in the front seat. On the way back to town, I berated him for his sloppy lookout skills while I watched the sun set over the mountains and pondered what Duke was going to unearth in the mine.

CHAPTER TWENTY-FOUR

REHASHING REHEARSAL

As SOMEONE WHO responds well to routine, I ought not complain about it. But I'm going to. I didn't feel like joining my colleagues and going over the day's highlights. Not that I minded hearing what others had been doing, but I was concerned that Duke would list my claim-jumping activity in his highlights. I had no inclination to include it—or the return of Boots's hat—in mine.

The luster was taken off my complaining after I read it was a form of bragging. *Please note how wonderful I am for having to endure what I have to endure.* My complaints are mostly weak bids for attention and praise.

I shut up and got on with it.

All the gang was at dinner except Duke. While we waited, Boots told us we were having a special dinner tomorrow at the Star restaurant and hotel and to get there on time. We waited a while longer, then Boots asked for our contributions.

Annie kicked off the proceedings. "I was taken with what Waddie Mitchell said. He grew up with other cowboys. They had to entertain each other with stories because there wasn't any TV or radio out there on the plains. They had to develop their own rhyme and meter to keep people interested. It's not what he'd have called poetry and that struck a chord with me. We aren't all comfortable with being called poets. We could play on that."

There was general approval and Boots made a note.

"Dale and I have a proposal," Roy said. "We'll be discussing tonight's hayride and bonfire tomorrow, but we want to do something special."

"Waddaya have in mind? Making s'mores?" Boots asked.

"Let's sing some songs."

"I'm for that," said Annie. "Plus, there are lots of campfire songs to choose from."

"We're partial to 'Happy Trails,'" Roy said.

"Of course you are," said Buffalo.

"That'd be perfect for the end of the show," said Cat.

"I agree. We all want happy trails," I said. "The hayride was mentioned in the program. I've only ever seen them in the movies. Any tips?"

"Bundle up," said Annie.

That's when Duke came huffing in. "Sorry I'm late. I got tied up."

"No problem," Boots said. "We were considering what to sing at the bonfire."

"How about Marty Robbins's 'The Hanging Tree'?" Duke said, and stared at me.

CHAPTER TWENTY-FIVE

HAYRIDE

BOOTS HAD US all signed up. After the ride, we'd meet at the park next to the convention center for some bonfire time. Which meant more storytelling and song-singing, along with s'mores-eating.

After dinner we got ready to climb onto one of the wagons tethered to horses that looked like they'd have preferred a night off. I was feeling the same way. Someone who's used to being out in sub-freezing temperatures might think nothing of it, but I'm from Southern California. We complain, I mean brag, when the temperature drops below the fifties.

I was willing to forego whining if I got to sit next to Cat. Not so if I ended up between Duke and Boots. I'd prefer to ask her and get rejected than to surrender to a worse fate.

She was talking to Annie. In Dodgertown, I'd wanted to flirt with a woman who was talking with someone else. I'd stumbled into that conversation only to be put in my place. Cat and Annie had become closer over the week and I didn't want to appear intrusive. *Slow down, don't rush*, I reminded myself and then promptly paid no attention.

"Hey, is it my thin blood or is it cold out here?"

"It's cold," Annie said. "We were hoping they have extra blankets."

"I'm with you on that. Do the blankets go on top to keep you warm or underneath so the hay doesn't poke your ass?"

"I don't see any blankets," said Cat.

"Come on, they have to have blankets," I whined.

"I've never seen them underneath," Annie said. "What made you ask that?"

"One summer when I was a teenager, my best friend and I visited one of his friends in Colorado. We had the, um, pleasure of helping them load bales of hay onto a trailer. It was hot and we had to wear long-sleeve shirts because the hay scratched us. Still, we ended up sunburnt, all scratched up, and worn out."

"That right there is why you didn't become a cowboy or a farmer," said Cat.

"You're right. Whatever fantasies I had about those career paths ended that day."

At that point, some people came over with a pile of blankets and told us to take one and hop on.

"Hey," I said, "why don't the three of us sit together and share? Since we've established that I'm not cowboy material, I don't mind admitting that one blanket isn't going to cut it."

"Me neither," said Annie.

"Let's all grab two," said Cat.

I had the good fortune to be under the covers with Cat. I also had the fortune to be under them with Annie. I was between them. Cat wasn't harboring any overt animosity, which was promising, but I needed to be an equal-opportunity hayrider.

Despite the gold rush, Elko wasn't spreading out. The hayride didn't have extensive territory to cover. The universe was full of stars and the half moon was emitting dim light. What there was to see was more attractive in the dark.

"I've yet to hear your readings and storytelling," I said. "Did Boots pick you because you're well-known poets and storytellers?"

"Cat can answer for herself, but Boots didn't pick me for my fame as a storyteller poet. No, he and I have another kind of relationship."

"Care to expound on that?"

"We were an item a long time ago. We met back when we both lived in Butte."

"Your being able to maintain a friendship is quite an accomplishment," I said. "That's a skill set I haven't mastered."

"I'm friends with all my ex-beaus. We may not sleep together anymore but that doesn't mean we don't get along anymore. And, you know, sometimes we go to the rodeo again."

"Lucky you," said Cat. "I've not had any success either. It's not that my relationships end badly. They just end."

I knew what she meant, but maybe she meant something else. I tend to take things personally so I took it as a kind of warning. A warning our departed cast members may not have heeded.

"What about you, Cat? Is Boots one your former beaus?"

"We met five years ago. In a bar in Missoula. He was selling jewelry, and we hit it off because my family has some history with that. Boots wears a lot of hats. But not beau."

"Nothing wrong with that," I said. "I wear a couple myself. I wish I had one tonight."

"Go pick one up. We lose almost half our body heat through our heads," Annie said.

"I almost got one the other day. If I'm going to get a cowboy hat, this would be the place to do it."

"I'll go with you to Capriola's—I know men have a hard time picking out clothes for themselves," said the wrong person.

"That's very kind of you. I'll keep it in mind. So, Cat, did he ask you here because of friendship or because of poetry?"

"The poetry of friendship," said Cat.

CHAPTER TWENTY-SIX

POST HAYRIDE

W E   D I S E M B A R K E D   A T   the park. A glowing fire was already surrounded
by people holding sticks and marshmallows. Perhaps they'd skipped
the hayride and gone straight for the warmth. Not being a foreplay
guy, I was envious, although I'd made inroads with Cat and was
keen to see if I could separate her from the herd.

Some people were meticulous with the browning of their marshmallows; others stuck them in the fire and let them burn. I'd prefer
to skip the meticulous toasting, but I'm not a big fan of charcoal. I
was sucking on sticky fingers when Dale and Roy came over.

"How'd you like the hayride?" Dale asked.

"I like traditions so that part was fun. I'd have liked it more if
it were fifty degrees warmer."

"Roy said the same thing. Hayrides are for the younger set. Thin
blood and cold nights don't mix well."

"I'm with you. I'm eager to see your performances but I'm not
up to date on cowboy poets. Are you both well known?"

"Heavens, no," said Dale. "Roy can spin a yarn. I'm more of a
tagalong, but I dug up a handful of old poems and stories to tell,
so I'm ready."

"So how come Boots picked you both?"

"We all go way back," Roy said. "After high school he and I enlisted together."

"It's reassuring to have longtime friends. I'm still in touch with a couple of guys I met in the service, although they live on the East Coast so I don't see them often."

"We don't get to see Boots often either as we live in New Mexico," said Roy. "And he's always on the move, though he's mostly a Montana–Wyoming guy."

"He does seem to have a restless spirit. Has he lived in other places?"

"You bet," Dale said. "I bumped into him in Odessa when he first got out of the service and was doing pickup work for rodeos."

"Pickup work? What's that?"

"The unsung heroes of the rodeo. They're the ones who look after the cowpokes once their ride is up. You never can tell what those broncos and bulls are going to do."

"Not the easiest job."

"A good pickup man is an artist," said Dale. "And the rider's best friend."

"How come you know that?"

"In my younger days," she said wistfully, "I did some barrel racing."

"That's doesn't sound easy."

"There's nothing easy about being a cowboy."

A woman ran up to the fire and shouted.

"Someone's been shot."

That was a mood breaker. A bunch of us followed her to a far corner of the park. Behind a clump of bushes lay Duke. People were shining flashlights on him but he wasn't going to be shining back. There was too much blood. Someone said they were a doctor and bent over him—confirming what we knew and what we didn't.

"He's dead, all right. Been dead for some time."

The sadness was welling up inside me. I hadn't particularly liked the guy but I hadn't particularly not liked him. After he saw me in the mine, he'd liked me less. But prior to that we'd smoked some Prairie Gold, and that's a bonding thing.

I wasn't the only one who was sad. People were sniffling and crying. I couldn't see Dale or Roy, but Gene was standing on the outskirts of the group and I walked over to him.

"This is bad," I said.

"Yup. Poor guy's been lying out here for a while. He deserved better."

What did that mean? Deserved to die in a better place or suffer a better fate?

"You know him well?"

"Nope. Met him here. He was an ornery guy."

"He was? I didn't get that impression."

"Yer kiddin'?"

"Not really. He was rough around the edges, so I can get his being ornery. If what you mean by ornery means what I mean by ornery."

"Means he was a horse's ass."

"Oh, was he a horse's ass to you?"

"Obviously. Wasn't he to you?"

"Well, he got upset with me. But he wasn't a horse's ass to me."

"Who wasn't a horse's ass to you?" Buffalo said as he came up alongside us.

"Duke. It isn't good to speak ill of the dead. But we kind of were. How was he to you?"

"He was one of those guys who got up on the wrong side of the bed every day. He didn't like being him."

"See?" said Gene. "What kind of shrink are you?"

"Not a very observant one."

CHAPTER TWENTY-SEVEN

DWINDLING SUSPECTS

Thursday January 31, 1985

I REMEMBER ONCE reading an obituary page and thinking I never wanted to see myself there. Then it occurred to me that I never would. It didn't give me any relief and I doubt it would have given Duke any to know his obituary hadn't ended up in the *Elko Daily Free Press*. There was a short article, though it didn't tell me anything new, not even a time of death. If he died during the hayride it would eliminate Cat, Annie, and me among others. If he died before, the field was open.

Duke—ornery or not—hadn't killed himself as no gun had been found at the scene. Someone may have discovered the body, seen the gun, and taken it, but they probably would also have taken his wallet and his keys and driven off with a trunk-load of Prairie Gold. I'd need to check whether his Caddy was still in the lot.

While Duke being killed for the dope was certainly a possibility, so too was being next on the list.

What had the victims done to get on that list? I doubted I was on the list, because I had no prior connection with any of the departed. But others had said they were strangers to each other.

There was only one apparent through line.

Boots.

These were his people and he hadn't assembled anyone for their poetic skill set. Everyone had essence of cowboy poet in them. Except me.

I'm used to people not telling me things. Even though I get paid to help people express their truth, for every truth someone tells me, there's others they're not sharing.

Boots wouldn't tell me what I needed to know because the consequence of telling me would be worse than keeping his mouth shut. At the mystery writers' conference, the organizer had been blackmailed. That's what had kept him quiet. Was the same thing transpiring here?

Any one of the remaining cast could be the perpetrator. It dawned on me I hadn't followed up on Maverick, who'd kicked off the murders. He may have faked his death and be lurking behind the scenes trying to even old scores.

All of the victims were men. Did the killer have a singular grudge against men? Or merely "men first" was the way they were going through their hit list?

I had to touch base with everyone and dig below the surface.

And I had to go back to the mine.

I called up Gus and asked him if he'd caught up on his sleep. He apologized profusely again and agreed to meet me at the convention center at ten. I asked him to stop by the hardware store, ask how long the average mine was, and buy batteries and enough string for me to make my way to the end and back safely.

I headed over to the parking lot to see if Duke's car was where he left it. It was. Evidently the killer hadn't driven off with it and the police had yet to track it down. I wanted to check out the trunk, but my breaking and entering skills were not that developed. Instead I revisited where Duke had been found.

The daylight revealed little more. It was on the edge of the park and isolated—a place I'd go to sneak a joint or make out with someone. What had lured Duke here? Was someone going to buy a suitcase? Or was he going to land a kiss? I couldn't see Cat opting in. Annie possibly. Dale was closest age-wise. What happens in Vegas stays in Vegas. Did the same hold true in Elko? Dale wouldn't be the first person to go behind a spouse's back.

I trust these unanswered questions reside in my subconscious and come springing to life when needed. More likely they just slip away.

As I neared the convention center, I ran into Hal Cannon. "Good morning, Hal. Remember me? Boots introduced us. I'm in his dwindling cast."

"Yes I do. How are you?"

"I'm fine. But we're all shaken by—I can't remember their given names—Duke's, Lone's, and Hopalong's deaths."

"In all my visions of the Gathering, I never imagined people getting killed. I'm going to say a few words this morning to everyone. I didn't before because Jason and Richard died at Stockmen's and I didn't connect it to the Gathering."

"We've all been wondering what the connection is. Any insights?"

"I wasn't familiar with Richard. I've met the other members of your cast here. I took it for granted they were all Boots's friends."

"He's the one connection I've found." I paused then changed the subject. "I want to congratulate you on putting this all together. I can tell it took a substantial amount of time and energy by a lot of people. I'd welcome hearing more about it. Do you have an office?"

"Drop by the museum in town. There's an exhibition of cowboy cartoons, illustrations, and folklore. They graciously gave us a room that serves as conference central. That's where I work when I'm not here."

"Thank you for the invitation. What do you mean by folklore?"

"It's the parts of history that come forward with us personally.

Folklore's culture. Like learning how to make jam from your mother, making quilts, or telling stories; the way we tell jokes, or the kind of music we appreciate. It's down-home, everyday people. There are no stars in folklore."

"There's much to be said for that."

"The exhibition will aid with your show. I'm surprised Boots didn't recommend a tour. I'll have to suggest it to him. Now, I have to go. Hope to see you later."

Hal had an ease about him, which would have helped him to persuade cowboys to come and share their stories and poems. Elko was chosen because it was a real cowboy town and January was a light month for cowboy work. That thoughtfulness went a long way. Would it go all the way to creating an event so Hal could take care of his grievances? I didn't want to believe that, but you're never sure when murder's involved.

CHAPTER TWENTY-EIGHT

OBSERVATIONAL SKILLS

I WANTED TO go inside, warm up, and listen to Hal address the deaths of Duke, Lone, and Hopalong. Instead Boots came up to me.

"We have to talk."

"Sure," I said, and turned toward the convention center, but he turned the other way, toward the park.

I got nervous as we approached the spot where Duke had been found.

"What's up?" I asked.

"I got two things. Notice anything different about me?"

I studied him. Steady brown eyes, high forehead, sunken cheeks, recently shaved.

"You used a different toothpaste?"

The more he was getting to know me, the less was his faith in my detective skills.

"I'm wearing my hat."

"So you are. Did you find it someplace?"

"Someone left it in my room."

"That's great. It's such a part of you that I didn't even notice."

"Yeah, someone put it in my room. Probably when I was doing

my show. Must have been someone who wasn't there. Any ideas who that mighta been?"

"Not off the top of my head."

"Yeah, well, I do. I'm not one to make accusations until I'm positive, but I'll get to the bottom of it."

"You want to be thorough. I'm happy to help out."

"I'm sure. Now, take a look. What else do you see?"

"It looks like it did yesterday. Trees and bushes, grass that's waiting for spring to perk up. I don't see anything unusual or out of place. What do you see?"

"The same thing. What I don't see is a reason to shoot someone. Not here. It's not that out of the way. The trees and bushes give a little cover but this isn't the place I'd choose to kill someone."

That relieved me.

"For what it's worth, here's something that's been simmering in the back of my head," I said, trying to gain a measure of respect. "Most cowboys have guns. Even cowboy poets. Our hotel's walls were not built for privacy. All night, I can hear the laughing, singing, hollering downstairs, and the people next door enjoying themselves more than I am. Yet I haven't heard gunshots. Anywhere. If Duke was shot out here in the open, wouldn't someone have heard it? We're not that far from the convention center."

"Someone either used a suppressor or dumped him here."

"Suppressor? You mean a silencer?"

"Yup."

"Do cowboys use them? Wouldn't it make it kind of hard to pull your gun out of the holster?"

"Yeah, but if you want to go hunting and not make noise, you need one. They're a hindrance in a gunfight, but we don't have those too often anymore."

"I guess if the killer hadn't brought one with them there's a place in town that sells them."

"Cowboys are crafty. I expect they made their own."

"Yeah, Dale and Roy were all gussied up in outfits Dale sowed."

"Cowboys are handy in all sorts of ways. We make rope out of horsehair when we need to. I bet most everyone here can make a suppressor. Although most of us don't use one coz when we go hunting we do don't require more than one shot."

"You do get to save on bullets," I said, hoping he wasn't planning on expending a round on me. "Let me ask you about Duke. Care to tell me why he was invited?"

"You figure it out. That's why I brought you out here."

We stood at the back of the large meeting. Everyone was standing and no one was wearing their hat. Hal was speaking.

"Our fallen brother was a good hand. He deserved a better fate. Let us take a moment to honor him."

People bowed their heads. I followed suit for a moment, then scanned the room. I was hoping to see someone smirking or otherwise disrespecting Duke, but mostly saw the backs of heads. I tried to focus on Duke and his loss. Most of us don't want to die and hope it'll come at the end of a fulfilling life. Duke hadn't had his fair share but since when has life been fair?

The morning's performances would begin soon and people drifted out of the room. Annie was on the program, and while I didn't want to be there, I should.

I've written before how we ought not *should on* ourselves. Albert Ellis, PhD, coined the term *shoulding* and suggested we turn the negative mindset of a should into a want. I tried to find the part of me that wanted to listen to Annie.

I got some help.

"That was lovely, what Hal said," Cat said. "Made me respect Duke in a totally different way."

"That's heartening," I said, and wished I'd heard more than I had.

"Cowboys are the salt of the earth. No stars. Just regular people living their lives with care and respect."

"Yeah, so often we focus on the stars and don't give the everyday down-to-earth the credit it deserves."

She frowned.

"Changing the subject," she said, "that's a tough act to follow. I want to see how Annie handles it."

"I'm sure she'll navigate it well."

I was sticking to basics.

"I'm going to go to the restroom. Shall we sit together?"

Things were looking up.

While I was waiting for Cat, Roy came over. "Hey, Slick. How you holding up?"

"I'm holding up. You?"

"I'm sorry for Duke. I don't want to see anybody shot but he may have had it coming."

"He did? Why do you say that?"

"He and I were over at Capriola's yesterday. He got into it with some people and, from what I could tell, he was way out of line."

"The clothing store?"

"Yep. Single best outfitters in the West. G. S. Garcia grew up in San Luis Obispo, home of the vaqueros—some of the foremost horsemen in the world. He was originally a saddlemaker and his customers were Nevada cowboys who trailed their herds to California for the winter. They kept telling him about Elko, so he came out here and set up shop in 1893. The rest is history."

"I may stop by and get myself a hat."

"Or steal Boots's."

Hmm.

"I wouldn't want to steal another person's hat. But tell me, what happened with Duke?"

"I didn't see the ruckus, as I was checking out the spurs. Theirs are second to none. Not that you have any use for them in LA, but out here they come in awfully handy and we get a kick out of showing them off."

"Yeah, I'll pass on that. But what about Duke?"

"All I can tell you is there were raised voices. And after a lot— and I mean a lot—of back-and-forth, he came up to me in a huff and told me we had to leave."

"I was told he could be ornery. Did you ask him what caused all the huffing?"

"That's the difference between you city folks and us cowboys. We don't pry into other people's lives. If he'd wanted to tell me, he would've."

"I get that. But I'm a city boy. What do you think happened?"

"I told you, he was out of line."

I can tell when I've crossed the annoyance threshold. It was time to take on cowboy ways and keep my mouth shut. Cat came back and the three of us went and listened to Annie.

CHAPTER TWENTY-NINE

SURPRISED

ANNIE INTRODUCED HERSELF, and started yodeling. I hadn't see that coming. She kept at it too. I'm not familiar with the nuances of yodeling but she covered the spectrum. There were moments I pictured a shepherd in the Alps and then a coyote howl put me out on the prairie.

When she finished, I clapped as hard as anyone.

Rock 'n' roll bands begin their sets with strong songs. Not their very best, but their upper tier. Annie peaked too soon. Her stories and poems didn't stand out; it was the yodeling that would linger with the audience. She mixed it in periodically and had the audience joining in. When she was done, she got a standing ovation.

Cat wanted to go talk with her. I'd have preferred her to stay and talk with me but at the same time I wanted Annie to be with those who wanted to be with her. Roy took off as well so I stayed in my seat and pondered what to do next.

I could go to Capriola's and see what Duke had gotten himself into, but that was a long shot. I could also get a cowboy hat, which would aid in the heat retention, but what would work for me in Elko wasn't going to get any wear in LA. Plus I'd feel like a pretender.

While I was hemming and hawing, Buffalo was leaving. He

was in a hurry so I followed him. He kept a fast pace as he entered the park. Was he the criminal returning to the scene of the crime? I slowed. Thankfully, he kept on going to the museum where Hal's office was located.

No one else was going in and I didn't want Buffalo to discover I was on his tail, so I waited.

I grew up in New York City and spent most of my museum time in the American Museum of Natural History. Of course, as with most things affiliated with New York, you can multiply your home town's anything by at least ten and maybe closer to a thousand to get into a New York state of mind.

What I valued in the museum in New York was what I valued in the Elko museum. There were exhibits of everyday life as it had been lived by our ancestors. The further removed we are from those days, the more grounding it is to be able touch back to our roots.

There were saddles and all manner of cowboy accessories, old black-and-white pictures of Elko back in the day when people didn't make it to breakfast. There was mining memorabilia, including photographs of prospectors whose prospects didn't look good.

But Buffalo wasn't touching back to his roots, at least not in any of the public spaces. I asked at the reception desk for directions to Hal's office, found it, and knocked on the door. There was no answer. A closed door doesn't necessarily keep me out. I stepped in.

We were equally surprised.

"What are you doing here?" Buffalo said.

"Funny," I said. "I was going to ask you the same thing. Well, actually, I was going to ask how come you didn't answer when I knocked on the door."

"I asked first."

"We're not going to play that game, are we?"

"I'm here on business and I didn't hear you knock."

"So I gather. In that case, I'm also here on business. Given that we're both here on business, let me ask you, how's business?"

"That's none of your business."

"Apparently. But how would I know if I didn't know?"

"You'd know when I stuck a two-by-four up your ass."

"I'd certainly know something. But I might misunderstand."

"Being a wiseass isn't always wise."

"So I've been told. But what are you going to do? You have to be you. So, come on, tell me what you're doing here and I'll tell you what I'm doing here."

"Now who's playing games?"

"I like to meet people where they're at. You want to play games, I'll play. You want to stick a two-by-four up my ass, well, I'm not inclined to want to go there with you, but I'll want to get even. So let's not do that. Let's help each other out. What are you searching for?"

"If you don't want to get out of here with that two-by-four up your ass, you need to leave now."

I couldn't see a two-by-four but I know when I've overstayed my welcome.

"Why don't we both go chat with Hal and ask him to help us out."

"You know what's good for you, you'll keep your mouth shut."

"I'm a big believer in holding confidences. That door swings both ways. I won't tell if you won't, but let's get out of here together. What do you say?"

He stormed out in front of me.

CHAPTER THIRTY

A NOONER

BUFFALO HAD NOW jumped to the top of my list of suspects. We left the museum and walked in silence—doing that cowboy thing where you're respectful of the other person's privacy. It's not my usual path but this time I took the prudent route.

We got back to the convention center and I bid goodbye to Buffalo. He went to the bathroom and I stood behind a display where I'd spot him leaving but he wouldn't see me. He came out and made a beeline to his Chevy pickup in the parking lot.

In for a penny, in for a pound. I hurried over to the taxi stand.

"What took you so long?" Gus said. "I've been waiting here for an hour."

"It's a good thing I'm not paying by the hour. Want to say what I'm going to say?"

"Follow that Chevy pickup."

"You got it."

"Were you able to get the string and bring a flashlight?"

"Of course. We going prospecting?"

"I thought we'd try to hit the mother lode."

"You mean someone else's mother lode."

wanted Roy to accompany her somewhere and after a short round of hellos and goodbyes they left. I was curious where. But not enough to follow. I had other things to do.

CHAPTER FORTY-EIGHT

BUFFALO TALK

Buffalo was in the lobby reading a bulletin board full of messages, flyers, and poems. "Hey, Buffalo, that was quite a performance you, Boots, and Gene pulled off in there."

"Thanks. We were having a drink the other night and Boots suggested we do our own version. Gene and I were unsure but people were enjoying it."

"I did, but there are purists who think differently."

"No one would think of Boots and me as purists. Gene's more down the middle."

"Purity can be overrated. I want to follow up on what you told me earlier. You said that you got a share to help out. What did you mean?"

"It was a poor choice of words. Whenever you get a share of something, you're helping out. But I've been wondering about the murderer—heck, we all have—and whoever it is doesn't have their head screwed on right. There's no logical reason for any of this."

"I'm a city boy, and you cowboys have a different code, but anyone who kills doesn't have their head screwed on right. Unless it's self-defense, but that's not what we're dealing with here."

"You're the shrink, you tell me. Whodunit?"

"That's the thing about crazy. Sometimes you can spot someone across the room and it's easy to tell some cards are missing from their deck. Other times not so much."

"Ain't that the truth. I thought my first wife had her act together till she came after me with an ax one night."

"Sorry to hear that."

"Not as sorry as me. She was the one with the money. She wasn't that crazy."

"Money and crazy can be well acquainted."

"I'm not well acquainted with it anymore."

"Money or crazy?"

"Come on, Doc. We're all crazy one way or the other, but we ain't all rich."

"That's true. So which crazy person did this and why?"

"Darned if I know," he said, moving away from the bulletin board and me. I stayed with him.

"Does it have anything to do with the shares?"

He hesitated. "Possibly."

"Come on, Buffalo. If you bluffed in poker like you just did, it's no surprise you ain't rich."

"Maybe it has to do with the shares, but I don't think so. What do you say?"

"I say maybe too."

"You being cutesy with me?"

"I suppose so. You being cutesy with me?"

"I suppose so."

"There you have it. Want to tell me what you were doing in Hal's office? Want to kick things up a notch or continue to dance around?"

"You boys fixin' to do some dancin'?" Cat asked.

"We were dancing around the topic of shares," I said. "We weren't doing any fast-footing."

"Slick was doing some fast-footing. I'm more of a slow dancer."

"Ah, Buffalo Bill, don't sell yourself short," Cat said. "I saw you up on that stage singing. You've got your moves."

"Thank you, young lady. We did have fun up there."

There are two opposite approaches to getting people to tell the truth. For the most part people are inclined to tell you a secret in private. But, a group induces peer pressure. Self-disclosure begets self-disclosure. If I could get Cat to share what she knew, Buffalo might share what he knew. Or it could work the other way as Buffalo and I had warmed up.

"Buffalo, can you tell Cat and me more about the shares?"

"If you know anything, you keep what you know to yourself, like I'm doing." With that he tipped his hat to Cat and nodded at me as he made his departure.

Non-disclosure can also beget non-disclosure.

CHAPTER FORTY-NINE

BRIBES

CAT AND I kept a brisk pace to the place I'd lunched with Dale. I endeavor to get a decent amount of fruit and vegetables into my engine, but ice cream is my first love and I was ready for a midafternoon pick me up. It's not a preferred winter snack and it has close to no nutritional value, but it works for me. I asked Cat if it would work for her and when she said, "You bet," her grade-point average with me jumped up again.

She opted for a scoop of vanilla and I for the trifecta—vanilla, chocolate, and strawberry.

My ice cream wasn't the only thing with a mixture of flavors. A part of me was trying to determine if she was the killer and a part of me was wanting to flirt with her.

"Cat, I've got a problem and I need some help."

Watching Boots, Buffalo, and Gene on the stage had given me a trail to follow to get the killer to reveal themselves, but more clues would help. And let's face it, my chances of solving the mystery were greater than my chances with Cat.

"Does it have to do with your ice cream intake?"

"That's a worthy topic, but no. This is something else."

"Shoot."

"It has to do with you and me."

"It does?"

"Yeah, it does. It's the last day of the Gathering. I'm slated to leave here tomorrow and drive home. You're going in a different direction. If we lived closer, I'd be seriously pursuing you, but unless you're harboring plans of moving to LA, I don't see a future for us."

"I see why you have a problem."

"Want to help me with it?"

"What would you like me to do? Aside from admitting I've been harboring LA fantasies."

"How about *Who needs tomorrow, we've got tonight.*"

"I could say that. It's crossed my mind."

"It has? That sounds promising. Well, sort of."

"Let's eat our ice cream, change the subject, and let things take care of themselves. We'll find out soon enough how they play out."

"That sounds so grown-up."

"Being a grown-up has some advantages."

"I don't have to sit in Madame Defarge's French class anymore. Since you suggested we change the subject, when we spoke earlier you said the killings were about greed and you wanted to set a few things right. Were you able to do that?"

"No. I had an idea, but I was wrong."

"Want to share it with me?"

"It was nothing."

"Does this have to do with the shares? You know more than you've let on. You willing to say more?"

"No."

"Okay. Let's put the shares thing on hold for the moment. Instead, tell me why people are reluctant to share more."

"Let's not go there."

"Everyone's loath to talk, but I'm betting the shares have a direct bearing on the murders. How can we uncover the killer if no one will open up?"

"You have a point."

"Thank you. How does this sound? Only talk about you."

"The reason others aren't talking is the same reason I'm not. I was asked not to."

"That's considerate of you. So you were asked not to tell. Who asked you not to tell?"

She smiled at me.

"I get that. But, come on, people say they won't tell all the time, but do. Why is this secret so special?"

She kept smiling.

"What if I told you I'd sleep with you? Would that turn the tide?"

She smiled a bit more.

"Can I bribe you?"

"Wasn't that what the ice cream was about?"

"That would work if you were trying to bribe me, but it hasn't been as effective with you."

"Give me some time."

CHAPTER FIFTY

COMPULSION

CAT AND I returned to the convention center. If you'd asked me to bet on how things would turn out at the end of the night, I wouldn't have known where to put my money. Our future was now or never. That saddened me. While I can still get it up for a one-night stand now and then, the lack of long-term prospects made this more bitter than sweet.

I don't always approve of how my mind works, but I'm stuck with it. As soon as I grasped that Cat and I might not spend the later part of the night together, Nina popped up. She held the strongest physical attraction for me, but there, too, lay the underlying knowledge that it wasn't going to work.

My reverie wasn't taking me any place I wanted to go, so I took myself to the room where Boots was again sharing his poetry and stories. Was having the stage to himself for a second time the opportunity he was thankful Hal gave him? He had an audience of fifty, including what was left of our cast.

He was making the best of the moment, though he didn't appear to be having any fun. I knew very little about the guy other than he'd didn't stay in one place for long and had earned himself jail time and a parole officer. Through it all, he'd stayed connected to the people who mattered to him—in much the same way Annie had maintained friendships with old beaus. But what kept him moving? Was he chasing the rainbow? Or running away from the storm? Probably the latter, given the themes of his poems and stories.

All week long I'd heard stories of life on the plains and the trials and tribulations of the cowboy way of life. But it wasn't so different for city folk. We all have to earn enough to keep a roof over our heads, food in our belly, and the bill collector away from the door.

In grad school, the founding campus dean, who was also a practicing psychologist, told us about a guilt-stricken client who loved to play cards and spent many hours every day playing poker for money. The dean asked him what he'd lost or earned over the years he'd been gambling. Turned out he made an ample amount, so the dean told him not to guilt-trip himself and make it his vocation.

What did Boots do for a living, aside from try to rob liquor stores? His poems indicated he shared a vocational path with the client. This refrain stuck with me:

Gamblers

some are optimists

some are realists

some are looking for salvation

some are going to play

until they have no more to pay

looking for death, so they say

driven by the compulsion of rage

Rage is an intense word. So is compulsion. Put them together, and you've got my attention.

Boots's poem told me he was aware of his gambling compulsion—*some are going to play until they have no more to pay*. If you've ever been to Vegas, or anyplace else where you can gamble, you may have walked away a loser even when had the option to walk away a winner. That happens to many of us—we don't quit until it's too late.

Was that what Boots had meant by *looking for death, so they say*? Was it gambling slang? Was his gambling killing him? And *driven by the compulsion of rage*—was Boots feeling driven to kill himself or was it making him want to kill others?

That's the thing about poetry, and why I don't embrace it much. It's oblique. I got enough of that going on already.

CHAPTER FIFTY-ONE

LAST REHEARSAL

I CALLED GUS and left a message for him to come join the audience for the finale; I may need to call on him. I also wanted to know where Cat had gone and what he'd found out.

I hadn't had any of those "Oh, they're the killer" moments you often get. I'd had "They could be the killer" moments, but no one was standing out.

I was at that place where I had to accept the limitations of my sleuthing skills. I get passing grades for collecting random pieces of information, lower grades for figuring out a solid clue versus a misdirect, iffy grades at putting it all together, and trophy-earning grades for reveals. The final grade is the most important, but I'm hoping to raise my overall GPA. In the meantime, to pass the course, I'd need to do some last-minute cramming.

"Tonight's the night," Boots said as we were eating dinner. "We've had a rough week and lost people who now live in our hearts. We've shared tears and laughs. We've heard stories, told stories, sung songs, and shared the poetry that is our lives. I said you'd get a copy of the script earlier in the day and I'm sorry. As is often the case in life, it turned out there was more to this than I'd realized. I'll go over the basics for tonight, then hand out the scripts. We'll have to make do with what we've got."

"Ain't that the cowboy way," said Gene.

That received some gentle whoops. If Annie had been there, we'd have done some group yodeling.

Boots outlined how the show would work. He'd introduce our characters, we'd make an entrance and line up on stage. After he shared an irreverent re-telling of the history of the Gathering, we'd read our parts. People would be heckling and he encouraged us to go off script and banter with the audience. Buffalo, Gene, and Boots would reprise "Riders in the Sky" and I'd close the show. We'd then have the audience join with us in singing "Happy Trails."

I had a trail to travel, but it didn't look like a happy one.

CHAPTER FIFTY-TWO

OPENING ACT

As I DROVE over to the convention center for the last time, I had a vague sense of how I'd pull it all together.

I don't refer to myself as an expert. I'm not even an expert in me, although I know more about me than anyone else. However, to pull off the kind of group-process, voodoo-therapy reveal that I do, others need to believe I know what I'm doing.

Problem was, I doubted the cast held that high an opinion of me. I'd have to go the Clouseau/Columbo route and depend on people underestimating me.

It's times like this I want to be able to call up Sherlock Holmes and have him tell me who the killer is. I don't have his number. And, being the guy I am, I want to figure it out myself.

So, let's go figure it out.

Hal Cannon was standing on the stage with other Gathering officials. He shared what a joy it had been to put the event together and how it had exceeded their expectations. They'd conceived it as a one-time event, but the owner of Stockmen's Hotel had made a substantial offering, so they'd come back next year. That got a standing ovation. Clearly business in Elko in January had gotten a boost.

A band came on and played "Git Along, Little Dogies," "El Paso," "Streets of Laredo," and "Pancho and Lefty." I tried to be in the moment and enjoy the music but kept hearing snippets of songs I might be singing at the end of the night.

When the music was over, Hal announced a short intermission. There was a bar set up in the lobby and business was brisk. I hoped it would get real brisk and loosen things up a bit.

After a time, the audience returned. Boots bounded onto the stage and had us wait at the back of the room.

"Good evening, ladies and gentlemen. Please allow me to introduce our cast. Joining us this evening are … Dale Evans."

Dale went skipping down the aisle, such as she could, to some hoots and howls.

"Roy Rogers!"

Roy twirled his gun and sang "Don't Fence Me In." The hollering picked up.

Boots pointed his hand and raised his voice.

"Why, here's Buffalo Bill."

Buffalo shuffled along with a hunting rifle looking very much the rough hombre he was.

"Who's that I see? Oh it's Gene Autry."

Gene strolled down the aisle, then as he climbed onto the stage he threw out his lariat and roped Boots.

"Don't look now but here's Cat Ballou," said Boots, slipping off the rope.

Cat was awfully inviting as she sashayed her way to the stage and pointed her gun at the more raucous audience members. She hit the high mark for hoots, howls, and whistles.

"Oh, and here comes Slick."

I hit the low mark for boos, sneers, and snickers.

"Boys and girls, this is our cast for tonight. We're going to review the week's highlights and you're welcome to shout out your own two bits coz we couldn't stop you if we wanted."

CHAPTER FIFTY-THREE

SHOW TIME—THE SETUP

SEEING CAST MEMBERS with guns put my blood pressure in dangerous territory. Seeing Sheriff Quinn, Deputy Dough, and Gus brought it down again slightly. Seeing Nina raised it again. She was wearing a suede jacket and a wicked smile. It was distracting and exciting all at once. Especially when she made eye contact and tapped an empty chair beside her. Things were definitely ramping up.

Boots shared his irreverent version of how the Gathering had evolved and we all contributed different highlights, and the audience had a fun time with it. I kept waiting for someone to mention the killings but they didn't. Boots had left that to me.

After we'd finished the script, Boots said, "And now we have a very different highlight that will surprise, amaze, confuse, and ultimately enlighten you."

He pointed at me.

It's not a good sign that people are disappointed when you show up. Though I nailed the surprise and confusion elements. Now I had to amaze and enlighten.

"Thank you, Boots. Before I begin, let's have another round of applause for our actors."

When that died down, I said, "We've had memorable highlights this week and it's great news about next year. Let's hear it for every-one who had a hand in making this such a special event."

That got some hoots and hollers. I needed to milk the audience a bit to get things stirred up.

"We're now going to create some poetry, though a different kind from what we've been listening to all week. I'll start with a line of a poem. Then I'll point to someone to create the next line. When they're done, I'll point at someone else. Maybe me. Maybe you. We'll see. Our poem, like all poems, will speak to the truth of the matter. We're going to put our collective poetic chops together to discover who killed the other members of our cast."

The room got awfully silent. Before anyone took us off course, I began.

"This is a poem about murders so foul."

I pointed at Boots. He sneered at me.

"There's a killer loose who's on the prowl."

Good one, I thought, and pointed at me.

"Who tonight will be revealed for the fates that they sealed."

I pointed at Buffalo.

"It's a story best told in its narrative form, as the bastard who-dunit has broken a norm."

I pointed back at me.

"Rules are made to be broken. Let's not restrict us as we seek to reveal who's trying to evict us. State what you want, however you choose, in rhyme or free verse, but the truth must be told, or the trail will go cold."

I pointed at Roy.

"People were killed for the shares that they held."

I pointed at Dale.

"Yet, that may not be why they had to be felled."

"That's true," I said. "We've yet to determine why those known to the cast as Maverick, Hopalong Cassidy, The Lone Ranger, John 'Duke' Wayne, and Annie Oakley were killed. But, take a look around you, the killer is in the room now and soon will be taking their very last bow."

That got some gasps and heads turning.

"But why would anyone want to kill five people—and conceivably be plotting to kill more? And who is that someone? Those are the questions we'll answer tonight. To do that, we need to go back in time. Roy, have you recently been to a gold mine?"

"Early in the week, just to take a peek."

"What did you see?"

"Gene Autry."

"That so?" I asked Gene.

"Yup."

"And what did you discover when you met there?" I asked Roy.

"There was a there there, but we didn't meet there."

"A there there? And you didn't meet there, but there you met?"

"Yeah."

"Gene, what exactly was the there there?"

"The mine was there. Right where it was claimed to be."

"Who told you where it was claimed to be?"

"Buffalo Bill knew the way, and said to go in the day."

"So was it happenstance that you met Roy in the mine?"

"It was to me. Can't speak for he."

"Why did you go to the mine?" I asked Roy.

"To see if there was a there there."

"Just so I'm clear, you went to the gold mine to see if the gold mine was there?"

"Yeah."

"That true for you, too, Gene?"

"Yup."

"Were you able to verify there was gold there?"

"Nowhere did I see any, but I didn't look aplenty," said Roy.

"How about you, Gene? You go searching for gold and find any?"

"Not so's I'd tell you."

I stood next to Boots. "Want to tell us about the gold mine? I bet you've got stories to tell."

Boots wasn't happy.

"I've been told it's all fool's gold. You search all day and sweat and pray. Soon enough you fold, buried in the cold."

"Those words hold the mold for a story we've been told," I said, feeling full of myself. "But here's the problem I have. I'm lousy at deciphering poetry. Yes, part of its allure is the obscure. Yet, that's not going to help us."

I stepped off the stage and over to where Hal was sitting. "Hal, we need your help. What can you tell us about Boots? How did he come to be the director of our show? Did he write you and ask, or what?"

"I'd been traveling throughout the country, trying to encourage cowboy poets to come and share their poetry, stories, and songs. But Boots, he found me. Yes, he wrote and asked if he could put on a show, and everyone would have a chance to perform on their own. I was thankful to add him and the cast to the program."

"That was kind of him to offer, and I hope everyone's enjoying it." That didn't get the hoots and hollers I'd pandered for, but if I've learned anything, it's important not to let other people's lack of enthusiasm slow you down. "Do you remember anything in particular in his letter that had to do with gold?"

"Now that you mention it, I do. He had his own fancy stationery. Bootstrap Mine, Elko, Nevada."

"Boots, you the owner of that mine?"

"I was. It ain't been nothing but heartache. I'm glad to be done with it."

"Sorry to hear that, but it must be a relief to have been able to sell it. When did you?"

He mumbled, "Buffalo better answer that."

"Buffalo, When was the mine sold?"

While I don't usually take comfort in other people's discomfort, I was enjoying Buffalo and Boots's.

I still wasn't sure how to tighten the noose, never mind whose neck to put it around, but we were getting closer.

CHAPTER FIFTY-FOUR

SHOW TIME—THE DELIVERY

I WAS AT the National Cowboy Poetry Gathering so I wanted to do my bit, but I ought to know better than to try to bring poetry into the reveal. My apologies. I'm better off leaving the poetry to the poets.

Members of the audience had begun to drift into the lobby. That didn't feel good till I remembered the bar was open and noticed they were coming back.

Buffalo had clammed up. Time for me to dip into my therapist tool bag and pull out shadowing. For a guy who disdains foreplay, it's a useful device because it usually helps move things along. And things needed moving along.

I came up behind Buffalo and got a contact high from the bouquet of moonshine.

"Let me assist you. I'm going to stand behind you and say what I think you're not saying. You can elaborate, correct me, or ask me to go away. I'm here for you."

He nodded in a way that said he doubted it.

"Here's the truth," I said as him. "I don't want to tell the truth, not because I'm shy or hesitant, but because if I do I won't be able to honor other people's privacy. I don't give my word to someone lightly and when I do I keep it." I glanced over his shoulder as if to ask, "How am I doing?" He didn't respond so I continued. "But people have been killed and if someone doesn't break the code of silence, we may never get to the truth. I apologize, but some priorities rise above others."

I paused. He stood still.

"The people standing up here, with the exception of Slick, have bought shares in Boots's mine and now we, along with others, are the owners."

I stood behind Dale. "I wished you hadn't said that Slick. Buffalo made me a promise. I didn't even let Roy know. Please don't do this anymore." I leaned over. She wasn't any too happy with me. Nevertheless, I carried on. "I did what I did for personal reasons. Reasons I don't want you to betray." She nodded.

I went over to Gene. "I'm not liking how this is going. If I wasn't standing up here in front of everyone, I'd hightail it out of here, but kick your ass first."

I didn't have to look closely—he might do that anyway. That didn't stop me from continuing as him, "What you don't appreciate is, like Dale, I had personal reasons for what I did and it's not what you think."

Even though I'd spoken as Gene, I agreed with every word. I needed someone to disclose those personal reasons, whatever they were, but who'd do that? Time to pull out the ace up my sleeve.

I climbed down off the stage and slowly, milking the moment, made my way to Nina. The closer I got to her the closer I wanted to get to her. I'd just as soon sit down next to her and let someone else close out the show, but that, too, was fool's gold. Instead, I stood by the empty seat. Not quite shadowing her but people would work it out.

"Hello, everyone. I recognize some of you cowboys from Mona's Ranch, and it's an honor to be here with you tonight. I've enjoyed the show so far, though I wasn't expecting I'd be performing in it. Not that performing has ever been an issue for me."

I snuck a peek. She gave me a wink.

"Slick asked me to be here because he found out I'm a shareholder too. There could be others in the audience are as well. Sheriff, Deputy, you holding any shares?"

Eyes turned their way. And theirs turned to mine.

"There may be other shareholders," I continued as Nina, "but what's crucially important is not that we have shares in the mine, but why we have them. Many of you aren't familiar with Boots. He's a complicated man who's been gifted with knowing how to be a true friend. There are only a couple of people in this world I can call a real friend. You do things for real friends that you wouldn't do for others. It's the right thing to do and it makes you feel the right way. Boots needed help, and like the rest, I helped him."

I returned to the stage and stood behind Boots, but before I said anything, he said, "What are you talking about?"

I scurried over behind Cat and answered. "You've been there for us in different ways at different times and, while I can't speak for others, this is payback."

I stood back in my place in line and said, "Boots, you're a good person who needed a helping hand. The gift of friendship you've shared over the years has moved these people to want to help you. That mine of yours is worth nothing, but your friends bought shares anonymously because Buffalo told them you were hurting."

"I don't know anything about this," Boots said.

I started to get behind Buffalo, who pushed me aside and said, "Old friend, you have a lot of pride and a lot to be proud of. But your demons have hurt you. You're a gambler. You bought the mine, fool's gold, but you rolled the dice. Every penny you've made you've gambled away. It was all I could do—sell shares in your mine to people who call you a friend. Shares that are worth nothing in terms of gold but worth everything in terms of friendship. We want you to step away from the mine, from the gambling, and take the stake we give you and settle down."

Would Boots bolt? The story Buffalo had told wasn't pretty and everyone in the room had heard it. For a prideful person this had to be excruciating.

I'd try to help.

"Boots, this can't be easy for you, but people care deeply about you and want the best for you. Everyone chipped in to help you, fully aware the shares they bought would solely profit you. Except one person. There's one person who bought their share seeking profit. That person was betting on the mine having value. That person knew Buffalo had called a meeting for tomorrow morning and whoever showed up would own the mine. That person discovered the mine was not full of fool's gold. And that's why they killed the others."

CHAPTER FIFTY-FIVE

ONE PERSON'S FOOL'S GOLD ISN'T NECESSARILY ANOTHER'S

You have to take chances in life. Some gamble in the casino, others in their love life. Some drive too fast, drink heavily, or eat processed foods; others, like me, play guessing games. I spend part of my working life trying to read between the lines. A client says she isn't sure what to do. I hear her uncertainty, but I also hear her mother's wishes and her dad's judgments. I work below the surface.

People had bought their shares not to take a chance on striking it rich but to help out a friend who'd gambled away too much of his life. Boots had invited his friends to have a fun time with him and perhaps nothing more, and Buffalo, ever his parole officer, had seen an opportunity to help him out.

Buffalo had put together a cowboy version of an intervention.

With the money, Boots could settle his debts and set himself straight. He'd have his friends' support and be asked to give up gambling. It wouldn't be easy, but when friends are there for you, it can make a difference. Interventions are similar to surprise parties except the gifts offered are compassion, concern, and an honest account of how you're messing up your life and need to clean up your act. Usually there's an abundance of emotion, an outpouring of love, and a trip to a place to recover.

That kind of activity was likely on the agenda for tomorrow.

But someone had gone their own way.

In the therapy world, people spend time digging up the whys of things. But knowing why is just part of the process. You still need to do something about it.

Why kill fellow shareholders? Greed? After all, with fewer shareholders, the bigger the share. Yet none of the suspects struck me as overly greedy. Maybe I'd been barking up the wrong tree. This may have less to do with greed and more to do with need. Boots might not be the only one in debt. If need was the hidden motivator, how would I bring it to light?

I stood behind Roy. "I don't get what's going on here. Yes, Buffalo contacted me and asked if I'd help out Boots, and I said without a doubt. We don't have extra money, but what's money for if it can't help out a friend? Boots did me a solid years ago and I'm in his debt. Buying the shares was a way for Boots to save face. Buffalo told me the mine wasn't worth a darn, but Boots wouldn't accept charity. This way, I'd help him without it seeming so."

I looked at Roy. He nodded.

"Roy, can you tell us why you didn't tell Dale?"

"Buffalo told me not to."

"Yeah, but there's more to it than that, isn't there?"

Roy was the strong silent type. Or at least the silent type.

"I'll tell you why," Boots said. "Roy and I have shared some things over the years, and it wouldn't have been wise for him to let Dale know he was helping me out."

"I can understand that," I said. "But Buffalo also asked Dale to help out and asked her not to tell Roy. Why'd he do that?"

"That door swings both ways."

"You did a solid for Roy, and you may have done a different solid for Dale?"

"Possibly."

I was tiptoeing. If I didn't up the ante we'd be here all night.

I went behind Cat. "I'm sorry this is all coming out, Boots, but hopefully it's worth it. You did me a solid, too, so even though it embarrasses you, we all have low points and I value you for being with me in mine."

Cat was staring straight ahead, waiting for the other shoe to drop.

"Money can be an evil thing and a wonderful thing," I said for Cat. "I know the evil part."

"Cat, let me ask you," I said, moving beside her. "Did you kill the other shareholders? It would give you a bigger share of the pot."

"If there was a pot," she said. "But Buffalo told us there was no pot."

"If the mine wasn't producing anymore, why would someone kill to get a bigger share? Are they going to build a subdivision out there or is the government going to do some testing? What's really afoot?"

Cat smirked. "You got it figured out?"

"Your family has some history with jewelry. Did you go in the mine, do some digging, and come upon the motherlode?"

"That's a reasonable theory but I've never been to the mine. Buffalo said it was worthless and his word's enough for me. What else you got?"

"Buffalo told everyone it was worthless and that Boots needed a leg up. Conceivably neither of those things is true. Buffalo may not be the good hand you judge him to be."

That got people taking a closer look at Buffalo. I didn't want to look his way and see him glare at me, especially as I hadn't pegged him for the guilty party.

"Boots, why are you so sure there's no more gold in the mine?" I asked.

"I don't want to talk about anything now, but that mine ain't brought in a penny these last years. There's nothing there but heartache."

"Thank you. One more question. Did Buffalo share any plans with you?"

"He encouraged me to put on this show and invite people I'd met along my travels who mean something to me. I told him I'd lost track of some of them, and he told me he'd track them down if I gave him the names. And he did. Well, most of them."

"What did you know regarding the shares?"

"Buffalo told me he was going to give all the cast members a share of something that had no monetary worth but would enhance their lives. But it was a secret and I couldn't ask about it or say anything."

"Thank you," I said,

I stood behind Gene. "Boots, I love you like a brother, but you're a fool. I've told you more than once what Einstein said. 'Doing the same thing over and over and expecting different results is insanity.' The reason you ain't found any more gold is you kept digging in the same place."

Gene made a face at me. I doubted Gene ever said such a thing to Boots but I needed to get that ball in play because someone believed there was gold in that mine and I needed to break them.

Gene didn't move so I got off the stage and slid down the row behind the sheriff and deputy and stood behind John Dough.

"I've got my eye on one of them. You got anyone sussed out for this, Sheriff?"

I stepped behind the sheriff. "I do. But I'm concerned. If they make a break for it, we're stuck in the middle of this row. I hope they don't get out of here before we collar them."

I scooched down the row behind Gus, put my hands on his shoulders, and said, "If they can't collar the killer, the rest of us will."

"You bet," he said. "Ain't no killer getting out of here tonight."

I wanted to get the killer searching for their exit. And to take it, quickly.

Scanning the room revealed too many people eyeing the exits.

Did the killer think I was on to them? Even if I couldn't easily put myself in their shoes, they must be very nervous. Anyone in that position wanted to be convinced they'd covered their tracks, but they'd be worried. Especially if everyone in the room was watching them and trying to discover if they were the guilty party.

I returned to my spot on the stage.

"We're going to wind things up now. I can assure you that in a few minutes the killer will be under arrest. That is, if the proper authorities can collar them."

I smiled at the sheriff and deputy. Neither had bothered to get up.

"Considering Nevada is a betting state, I'd like everyone except you, Boots, to place a bet on whodunit. Once we wind things up here, you can brag you knew it all along. In the meantime, turn to the people beside you and place your bet on who's the killer."

People started chatting. I turned toward my fellow cast members and looked each one in the eye. No one cracked. I was kind of hoping someone would bolt, but that would have made it too easy.

"Okay, everyone," I said multiple times to quiet down the crowd. "I'm going to ask the people on the stage to place their bets and state their reasons. When they're done, I'll let you know whodunit."

Boots was at one end of line. I went to the other.

"Roy, who do you hold accountable for these murders?"

"This is very unusual."

"You're right. It is, but let's do it anyway."

"I'd like to go last."

"Very well. How about you Dale? Who's the killer and why?"

"Gene. I've never trusted him."

That got some awkward applause from the Gene voters and some boos. It may have been a mistake getting the audience involved.

"Care to say more?"

"I've said plenty."

"Gene, what do you say?"

"I don't cotton to any of this."

"I can't imagine anyone does, but we're trying to focus in on the killer."

"If you know who it is, why not say so?"

"I would, but there's one more thing I need to confirm, and by the time we've finished, I'll have found it out."

Of course, I had no idea. You know that. But what you know and I know is thankfully not what the killer knew, and I wanted the pressure to build.

"Come on, Gene. Who's the killer?"

"You said someone in the room, so I say you."

That got hoots and hollers.

"Want to say why?"

"Cuz you're slick and full of shit."

That got more audience appreciation.

"Thank you for sharing. There's some truth in that. What do you say, Cat? Want to put your suspicions out there?"

"I don't want to, but I will since you said there was something you'd hear that would cement things for you. I'm picking Buffalo. I can't wrap my head around a parole officer with a heart of gold. He has an angle on this that we aren't seeing."

That got its share of heckles and taunts.

"Buffalo, you're next. Want to point out who you've got an eye on?"

"It's cruel of you to do this to us."

"As many of your parolees can attest, justice can be cruel. Who do you have your eye on?"

"The deputy did it. He's been a deputy for a long time. He's been passed over for sheriff. I wouldn't be surprised if the bullets match a gun he took off a crime scene."

That evoked catcalls, more taunts, and hollering.

If John Dough didn't do it, Buffalo ought to get out of town in a hurry.

"Boots, that leaves you, and Roy back at the beginning. I don't want you to make a bet so I'm going to pass it on to Roy."

"Don't do that. We ain't gambling for money. We're gambling on catching a killer and I want a turn."

"Suit yourself."

"I don't get along with any of this, but I do have a hunch. I want Roy to go before I say my piece."

"Roy, it's your turn."

"I don't care for this either, but it's clear to me that Cat did it. Seems to me she has money problems. She's not taken off running because no one would suspect her. But I do."

That got more brouhaha.

It was definitely a mistake getting the audience involved.

"Boots, we don't have an overwhelming favorite. You want to swing the tide?"

"Answer this first. Did you hear what you needed to hear?"

"I did. Did you hear it?"

"I did. I wasn't sure at first what you were talking about, but I'm a betting man. I admit I have a problem and need to give it up. But I want to bet one last time. I do know who did it."

"Nobody move," Roy said, drawing his gun. "They all deserved to die. I'm not a killer, but when someone breaks their vows they need to pay."

He turned and aimed at Dale. "I loved you. You betrayed me. You made me hate you. I killed them all because of you."

The sheriff and deputy pulled out their guns and pushed their way into the aisle.

Roy was in his own world—just him and Dale. They quietly stared at each. A deep calm came to his countenance ... the calm that often comes when the truth is aired.

Then he turned the gun toward himself and ended his life.

CHAPTER FIFTY-SIX

POST SHOW

"I'D HAVE LASSOED him if he'd tried to run away," Gene told me in the chaos that followed.

That was somewhat reassuring as the sheriff or deputy wouldn't have gotten there in time to save the day.

It was gruesome on the stage. I'd never seen anyone shoot themselves, nor the residual effects. Dale had been splattered with blood as she'd fallen to the floor moaning. People had gathered around her and soon the stage was full. Others had gone out to the lobby and the bar. It was a helluva way to end the Gathering—one they wouldn't want to repeat.

People wanted to congratulate or condemn me, but I had other things on my mind. I wanted to check in with Boots, Cat, Nina, and the rest of our crew. Mostly in that order. But there was little order in the universe at that time. They were surrounded by others who wanted to speak with them. I waited and decompressed.

I've had this feeling before. I'm in my moment of glory but there's no glory to be had. I didn't think well of myself for putting Boots in the spotlight, or having everyone point the finger at someone else and be taunted by the audience. No good had come of that, except the greater one of having found the killer.

Having Roy confess and then kill himself was gruesome. Yes, a jury would have found him guilty and sentenced him to death or life imprisonment, but somehow that would have been easier to deal with. Ending your own life that way is punishing. Roy's demons were punishing him as he had punished others.

Dale had said she and Roy met in high school. Feasibly, while he was in the army, she'd gone out on the rodeo circuit and done barrel racing, among other things. My guess is she was bucking other broncos, and that had weighed on Roy. Like Boots and Annie, maybe she'd kept up with some of her old flames, even fanned new ones. She did enjoy those looks she got when we walked down the street. I doubted I'd hear any of that from her, but if I were standing behind her that's what I'd be saying.

I understood why Dale's "betrayal" had driven Roy to kill her lovers. I didn't agree with it, but jealousy can cause you to do things you otherwise wouldn't do. Either Dale and Annie had had their own dalliance or Annie committed some other sin. Roy had lived by a strict code, one that constrained and tortured him and the people who broke it. He wasn't a sinning man, but he dealt with Dale's sins in a sinful way, which must have tormented him all the more. I wondered when he killed if he told his victims why and how they felt about the reason.

When Roy found out who Boots had invited, his suppressed resentment boiled over. To have so many of Dale's ex-lovers in one place was more than he could bear. People had sinned and while he couldn't kill his wife, he avenged himself on those who'd tempted her to break her vows. He'd been her judge and handed out the sentences.

Without Roy able to tell his story, we were all free to compose our own. Perhaps Maverick had been Dale's latest romance, and when Roy found out, he began his killing spree. Or Boots told Roy who was coming and that lit the fuse. There were questions answered and unanswered questions.

I was mostly waiting for Cat or Nina, hoping for one last grab at the brass ring.

A cluster of admirers circled Nina, and Cat was nowhere in sight. Boots was standing off to the side with Buffalo. I made my way over. Neither seemed pleased to see me.

"Gentlemen," I said, "it's been quite a night."

"You ruined everything," Boots said.

"I'm sorry you feel that way. I know I messed up some things, but not everything."

"You screwed me over—that's what I care about."

"Wait a minute, my friend," Buffalo said. "While Slick here did screw stuff up, he tried to do right by you. I don't approve of his methods and he made your private concerns public, but he did get Roy to confess and put an end to the killings."

"Tell that to Roy."

"Boots, I'm sorry that things you'd have preferred remain private were made public. It was never my intention to shame you. I only wanted to find out who'd killed your friends, and I couldn't conceive of another way to do it."

"Your intentions weren't bad, but I wish you'd talked to me first."

"I don't mean to be defensive—well, actually I do—I did try to talk to you. But you told me you couldn't talk to me. No one would. Buffalo asked everyone to respect your privacy, and they did. Buffalo even lied to me about the shares. I didn't want to do that dog-and-pony show up there, but I couldn't come up with other way. I'm truly sorry."

"That don't undo what you did, but I accept your apology. Now, we have things we need to discuss because I got other people to lay into."

"Before I go, I want to thank you for saying you saw the tell. It tipped the scales."

"You're welcome. He did kill my friends."

"You were bullshitting so that was very well played."

"I wasn't bullshitting."

"What? You saw a tell? I was bullshitting. What did you see?"

"For a bullshitter, you have a lot to learn. Now, it's time for you to go."

"All right. Thank you again for inviting me. I hope you're able to work things out for the better."

CAT STILL HADN'T put in an appearance and the crowd surrounding Nina wasn't any thinner. I got in the queue. I wanted to thank her for coming, looking ravishing, and helping out. And to flirt with finishing the night with her. But I wouldn't. For several prudish reasons, she'd already been relegated to my fantasy life.

It's ego-gratifying when an attractive woman sees you in a crowd and makes a point of coming over. Maybe it would be a late night. How uptight was I? As you can see, I'm a conflicted man. My resolve can turn from well-built to washed away in a moment.

"Hey, Slick, that was some show you put on."

"Thanks. I'm not sure that's a universally held opinion."

"You caught the bad guy. What else do they want?"

"They wanted more of their secrets staying secret."

"Isn't that what you shrinks do, unwrap secrets?"

"Yeah, but usually the client is asking for help."

"They'd be asking for help if Dale had screwed them over too."

"Possibly. But I wish I'd have found a different way."

"Feel free to beat up on yourself all you want. You coming over later for a nightcap or is this goodbye?"

"I'm honored you asked. There are any number of guys here who'd jump at that invitation."

"But you're not one of them."

"I'm taking you home with me and letting you live in my fantasy life."

"Your choice. They probably won't invite you back here, but if they do, drop on by. Let me give you something to give you a hand with those fantasies."

And with that she gave me the kind of hug that made me regret my choices.

I was relishing the afterglow when Hal Cannon came over.

"Well, you certainly ended the show with a bang."

"Yeah, I'm sorry. I wasn't expecting that."

"Don't apologize. You got the killer to confess, and while people don't want their secrets shared, you did what had to be done."

"Thank you."

"I do have one regret, though."

"What's that?"

"I'd asked Boots if I could join you all on stage at the end of the show for 'Happy Trails.' I'd have enjoyed that."

"That's too bad. That would have been a sweet way to end things. Or not, given that Roy Rogers turned out to be the killer."

"Yeah. I'll save it for next year."

None of the cast were at the convention center so I left. Gus was standing by his cab.

"Hey," I said.

"Hey yourself. Lucky was right about you. You have some skills."

"Thanks."

"Glad I could do my part. Lucky told me to be prepared for anything, so I was, but you had everything covered."

"Appearances can be deceiving. Thanks for showing up tonight. It was reassuring having backup if I needed it. Speaking of which, where did Cat go when you followed her."

"Over to Mona's. She stayed a bit and then left and came back."

"She wanted to set something right. Not sure she did, but glad you were able to follow her and show up tonight."

"My pleasure. Besides, aside from the shooting, it was an entertaining evening."

"Nice to know it was for someone. Thanks again. I'm going

back to my room. If you call up the hotel and leave a message for me with your address, I'll mail you a check."

"Thanks. If you come back next year, look me up."

As I drove back to the hotel, I sensed an exhausted fitful night's sleep ahead replaying events in my dreams.

I entered the lobby, and there was Cat.

"I was waiting for you. I had to get out of there but I wanted to see you before I went to bed."

"I wanted to see you too."

"You're a hard one to get a handle on. At various points this week, I've toyed with moving to LA."

"Wow. I'm honored."

"But I won't. Not after tonight. I don't like you anymore. Well, not in the move-to-LA way that I did. What you did tonight was cruel. People were hurt. Me, Dale, Boots, even Roy. You made us tell secrets we didn't want to tell."

"Yeah, I'm feeling pretty lousy about it, but I couldn't put it together any other way."

"You do what you gotta do. On the one hand, I respect you, but on the other, I care for you less."

"That's hard to hear."

"It's hard to say, because I'm still interested in you."

"Even if you cared more for me I just can't see a path for us. It makes me sad."

"I'll get over not liking you in a few days, and then I'll miss you. Here's my phone number. If and when you get sick of LA, or when you want some down-home country living, give me a call."

With that she gave me a hug that would also linger, and then walked away.

I settled in my room, too many regrets running rampant in my head. When I caught sight of the clock, it was exactly midnight. I remembered how I'd wondered which song I'd be singing at the end of the night. I didn't know the words to it, but *High Noon*'s "Do Not Forsake Me" seemed about right.

This is a work of fiction, which means I've taken liberties. In 2018 I heard about the National Cowboy Poetry Gathering and thought it would be fun to attend. The first book in the Lesson series takes place in 1977, and the next four in the early eighties. I have yet to tackle time-travel, so I knew this book had to take place in the same time frame, and that meant making some compromises. The Gatherings of the eighties, much like you and me, are not the same today, and for those who like their history more fact than fiction, this book may disappoint. Nevertheless, I've done my best to retain the spirit of the inaugural Gathering, despite the poetic license. All the characters are of my imagination except Hal Cannon and I made up most everything about him.

If you'd like a peek into what the future holds for David, take a look at what comes after the Acknowledgments and Apologies.

ACKNOWLEDGMENTS AND APOLOGIES

First off, I need to thank Hal Cannon. He was gracious with his time and allowed me to ask all manner of questions about the creation of the inaugural Gathering, which did take place in 1985. A few hundred people came to listen to some forty cowboy poets and "ranch folk" recite their own and classic cowboy poetry. The event was free and lasted three days. I stretched it out to five and added some activities. Many consider Hal the primary force behind the Gathering's inception, but he was quick to point out how many were involved and that he was glad to open the door to a lot of great talent. I've done my best to show him and the Gathering the kind of respect that's a central component of doing things the cowboy way.

When I told Hal the book was a mystery, he wanted to know if he got bumped off. I told him it wasn't in my plans, nor was having him be the one whodunit. When I start these books, I don't know what's going to occur and who does what to whom, so I was glad when he made it to the end of the book intact. He's still around, and if you're not familiar with him, you might want to check him out, and the National Cowboy Poetry Gathering.

I also want to thank Meg Glaser of the Western Folklife Center, which sponsors the Gatherings and was a force behind its creation. Most of the factual statements I make about the Gathering and Elko are based on Meg's and Hal's contributions.

I need to apologize for using the word cowboys as it's a non-inclusive term. Like *policeman* and *mailman*, *cowboy* needs to recede into history. Cow people, cow folk, or ranch folk don't roll easily off my lips and certainly didn't in 1985, but those terms are a step in a better direction as we move away from gender-based stereotyping.

I'm fortunate to have two close friends who are poets. Like most of their ilk, poetry writing has not precluded them from having other day jobs. Over the years, Steve Roth and Joaquin Shelton have both helped me to appreciate a poet's point of view, and I have quoted their verse in full or in part in this book. In truth, I would never have written this book if it weren't for them.

Stuart Bloom has brought his own poetic presence into my life. Ever since he brought the lyrics to "Tangled Up in Blue" to a poetry class we took in graduate school, he's been a guiding light in my life.

I asked some people how to cowboy up my dialogue so the characters would sound like someone other than me. Vivien Cooper was instrumental in giving me some guidance that allowed me to make things sound a bit more realistic.

Once again, the artwork was done by Chrissy and the artisans at Damonza. Their imagery always delights me and captures a certain essence of my stories.

Once again, thank you to Jake Robertson for bringing voice to the book and to me. He's taken my words and given them a life of their own.

And once again, if the book has held together well and flowed seamlessly, you can thank my editors, Lulu Swainston, Cally Worden, Beth Hamer and Ursula at Owl Pro Editing.

A LESSON IN COMEDY AND MURDER

INAUGURAL COMEDY CONFERENCE

DAVID UNGER, PHD

PROLOGUE

"THE BEST? THAT'S tough. First off, I don't remember that many, and those I do remember aren't necessarily the best."

"I can listen to your excuses only so long. When you're ready to play the game, let me know."

"Jeez. Lighten up. I'm just trying to think of the funniest joke I ever heard. It's not like we're building up to anything that's going to change the world."

"You can keep stalling. You're right, they're not going to drop a nuclear bomb on Palm Springs and destroy this epicenter of comedic talent."

"More likely we'll implode."

"Exactly. So come on—let's hear it. You can change your mind the second after you say it, but put up or shut up. What's the funniest joke you can remember right at this very moment?"

"Okay, okay, okay. It's not the funniest, but it's the first one that comes to mind. It's actually not a joke per se. It's something that happened recently and it gave me the biggest laugh I've had in a while. I was standing in the backyard of Joey Bishop's house ..."

He paused, milking the moment, trying to drag out however many status points he could garner from being at Joey Bishop's house.

"I'm drinking a lemonade. It's afternoon and I'm standing on the patio, talking to Joey about this very event. The backyard is full of friends, family, kids, and his two dachshunds. We're talking and one of the dogs is resting in front of us, and all of a sudden the dog starts licking its private parts. I look at Joey. He looks at me. We look at the dog, and I say, 'I wish I could do that.' And Joey says to me, 'You'd have to pet him first.' I tell you, the lemonade came flying out of my mouth. That guy is one of the funniest."

I wasn't drinking any lemonade as I waited in the reservation line to check in to the hotel, but I did laugh. Which I took as a good sign.

It was March 1985, I was at the inaugural Comedians Conference in Palm Springs, California, and I was getting paid for being there.

I don't know what comes to your mind when you think about a conference for comedians, but I thought there'd be plenty of funny stuff going on and no shortage of depressed people.

And, since it was a conference and I was there, maybe there'd be a murder or two.

CHAPTER ONE

THE BACKSTORY

I ATTEND MY share of conferences. I used to go in the hope I'd learn something and perhaps have a little romance too. Usually in reverse order. I still go to learn, and I still hope for romance, but the killings at a sex conference I'd attended shifted my mindset; now I'm also waiting for the shoe to drop. Or rather the bodies.

I'm a big believer in hope. With hope, you have a chance. Without it, you give up. I go to a conference hoping murder won't happen. But wishes don't always come true. Since I'm also a believer in going with the flow, if and when there are murders, I stick things out. It's not my fault they happen and the best I can do is help solve them and later write a book about it.

You know, you try to turn lemons into lemonade.

Turning lemons into lemonade is kinda my job description and why I was being paid to attend. The promoter wanted to create an environment where comedians and people who enjoy comedy could come together to celebrate the joy, art, craft, and business of comedy. He promoted the conference as an opportunity for aficionados, fans, and working comedians to come together for a week to learn, laugh, and live healthier and happier lives.

There would be a week's worth of workshops and playshops

on various aspects of the comedic arts, as well as comedy-making laboratories and comedian showcases. There would also be lifestyle workshops and a range of holistic-living activities. That's where I came in. I'd been asked to run a daily therapyesque workshop for interested parties.

Why?

Because I wasn't the only one who thought there'd be some viable candidates in attendance.

The organizer, Logan Macintosh, had contacted me, saying he'd heard good things about me from his friend Bennett Price, a *New York Times* bestselling author of mystery books. Bennett is also an on-again-off-again client who'd hired me to be with him while he attended the Mystery Writers of America annual conference in Las Vegas.

Logan and Bennett had spent a night on the town and got to talking about the comedy conference. Bennett had recommended me, not only because I'm a therapist, but also because I write a mildly amusing mystery series. Plus, I have some special skills that, if called upon, might come in useful.

Like the rest of my clients, Bennett calls me up when he thinks I could be helpful. After our week in Vegas some seven months earlier, he'd taken a therapy hiatus. Just recently, he'd called me up to book some sessions. Then Logan had offered me the job and Bennett starting gushing about our being at the conference together. That prompted a discussion about our professional relationship.

Professional boundaries are a dicey topic. I was in Vegas with him as his therapist. Yet we'd smoked a joint together and I'd assisted him in purchasing some cocaine. (I just need to take a moment here to remind the Board of Behavioral Science Examiners, who oversee my profession, that occasionally I resort to using my literary license.) I'd also almost conspired with Bennett in covering up the death of Louise, a Vegas brothel owner. Fortunately, she wasn't actually dead so I hadn't engaged in any deception.

Logan had invited Bennett to give a talk about comedy in mysteries since there are a lot of funny asides in his rough-and-tumble private-eye series. In Vegas, he'd wanted me to help him manage his nerves about presenting, but now he was ready to go it alone. Still, he was glad I was there, just in case.

Bennett figured that since we were both presenters, our therapeutic relationship would be on hold for the week and we could just be friends.

I gave him the standard therapist response: I'm your friendly therapist, not your friend. In fact, there isn't much difference when you get to the heart of it. Your friends are sometimes there for you when you need them and so too is your therapist, although usually more in spirit than in body.

In Vegas, he'd hired me, so he'd been my client the whole time. He hadn't hired me to support him in Palm Springs, though I'd seen him the previous week and we had plans to see each other the following week. The buddy-buddy thing for the in between week wasn't going to work.

Then again, when you've smoked a joint with someone it's not like you aren't already buddy-buddy.

Made in the USA
Columbia, SC
11 March 2023